Amy Har

THE CURSE OF
SCARLET

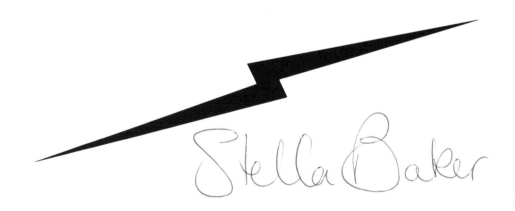

Stella Baker

Illustrated by **Nigel Baker**

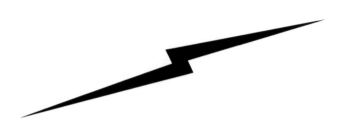

Typeset in Minion Pro

Editing, design, typesetting and publishing by UK Book Publishing
www.ukbookpublishing.com

ISBN: 978-1-913179-75-5

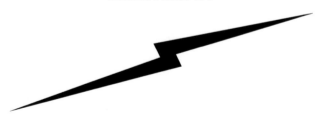

Amy Harrington &
THE CURSE OF
SCARLET

CHAPTER 1

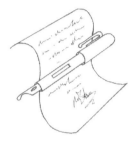

Always Trouble

*A*my Harrington had been excited about tomorrow, but now she was dreading it.

A letter had arrived addressed to 'Mr and Mrs Harrington (and Amy)'. The writing was thin, scratchy and spidery. It made Amy shudder.

At the worst possible time, mysterious Great Aunt Scarlet had written to announce that she was going to arrive for a visit.

And Amy knew about people like great aunts. Everyone would have to be on their best behaviour.

The letter had appeared without warning. "Dear Helen, David and Amy, I will be coming to stay…"

And there had been absolutely no question of whether it was a convenient time or whether they would be pleased to see her. Great Aunt Scarlet had just invited herself—with precise details of when she would be at Exeter station and insisting that someone should be there to meet her.

The truth of it was that no-one was looking forward to the visit. Helen and David, Amy's mum and dad, didn't say too much about it at first, but Amy knew for certain that they were not happy. And as for Amy, a girl who is soon to be twelve should be able to get together with friends to organise a birthday party, without someone arriving to ruin everything. It meant that the plans she had made with her best friends, Charlotte and Simran, were almost certainly going to be spoilt.

And that wasn't the only thing.

As the visit came nearer, Helen shared a growing worry.

"There's always trouble," she said. "Always some disaster just around the corner when Scarlet is near."

Amy asked her mum what she meant but Dad had shot her one of his 'don't ask' glances and shaken his head, so it was all still a mystery.

David had replied to the letter quickly and tried his very best to stop Great Aunt Scarlet coming to their home, but it was no good. She had made up her mind and when she had made up her mind—apparently, that was that.

Amy wondered why this aunt, that she had never met,

wanted to come to Boswell village anyway? Maybe she just
wanted a holiday by the sea.

Well, thought Amy, during the evening before the visit,
maybe it won't be so bad. Maybe Great Aunt Scarlet would
be a sweet little old lady in a knitted hat and sensible shoes.
Probably the sort of old lady that would smell of pear
drops and someone who might get tired easily and be in
bed by eight o'clock and fast asleep.

She decided to stop worrying about it tonight. It was
just a nuisance she was coming, that was all.

It was starting to get dark outside, but the summer
night was calm with not a breath of wind.

After a busy day at school, Amy had washed her hair
and changed into her night clothes. She crossed to the
window to close the curtains. Low and strange gloomy
clouds were slowly starting to gather. Amy hated the dark.

As the tall oak clock on the landing chimed, she
swished the curtains to shut out the shadowy sky and
concentrated on combing her long hair in front of the
mirror. It smelled of peach shampoo and felt smooth as the
comb ran through it.

She looked at the streak of white on the left side—a
wide strip of white hair in amongst the strong auburn
colour. She had never been able to understand why it was
there. She had even tried to dye it, but the colour just
wouldn't take. The white stayed as vivid as ever.

She turned her head a little and focused her eyes on the
side of her neck and the deep blue line just under her skin.

It started behind her ear, ran across her collarbone to the top of her right arm and then all the way down to the tip of her biggest finger. It was a bit like a vein but not quite. It couldn't be a vein if it went all the way down her arm in such a perfect straight line. She'd even had it checked out at the doctors. They said they didn't know what it was— but probably nothing at all to be concerned about. She'd had it since she was born. Sometimes it tingled a bit—like a tiny electric current—but it didn't hurt or anything. Just another odd thing. Like the white streak in her hair.

Was she imagining it, or was the blue line looking even more blue tonight? It was definitely tingling. And much stronger than usual.

Amy sat on her bed then leaned over and plugged in the hairdryer. She brushed her hand across the smooth pink bed cover.

The noisy dryer blew her hair out sideways. She closed her eyes and let a stream of warm air blow across her face. She loved being warm. It felt safe.

She took her time. When it was nearly dry, she started her nightly check for anything nasty—like a ghost or a monster lurking in her room.

Looking under the bed was always the worst part, so she put it off and checked the wardrobe first.

The wardrobe was pink but a different shade to the bed cover. It was small and cute with a metal key and a picture of a sweet baby deer on the door. She had named him Neddy-Knock-Knees because of his big knobbly knees.

She'd had the wardrobe since she was a little girl and she still liked Neddy. She loved his little brown body, spotted with white, his huge eyes and beautiful long eyelashes. She loved his skinny, spindly legs, his fluffy tail and his big gentle ears with soft dark fur on their tips. She loved the tall broad-leaved trees behind him in his little world.

Amy stood up, walked slowly towards Neddy, giving him a smile, and then turned the key and flung the wardrobe door wide open. No witches or a monster or a ghost so far. Just a neat pile of blankets with their flowery smell, two school shirts, trousers, skirts, tee shirts and her new blue jacket. Good.

Now the bed. But maybe the space under the desk first. Amy straightened the jumble of books on top and shuffled her science homework into a neat pile. She pushed her laptop along so that it was touching the wall. Not much to do. She had already tidied up, ready for her friends' visit tomorrow.

Amy plucked up courage and peeped behind the curtains. The sky was turning dark and not very nice for someone who is scared of darkness. No stars, no moon— just low unpleasant clouds. They looked menacing. Amy pressed her hand against the cold glass and dared herself to look up into the night.

It was then that she heard the sound.

CHAPTER 2

The Monster

She whirled around. What on earth...?

The sound came again. A scraping and a low growling.

Amy's bedroom door burst open and there he was—the terrifying monster.

"Oh, Barney—you idiot," Amy said, as the soppy little poodle jumped up at her. "I thought you were—well, I thought you might have been a scary thing."

Barney jumped up again. Amy giggled as they tumbled down together onto her bed.

"Well, now that you're here," she said, "you might as

well keep guard while I check under the bed and then, if anything comes out—you can eat them up—is that a deal?"

Barney's tongue lolled out of his funny grinning mouth and Amy hugged his soft black bouncy coat. He had a doggy smell all of his own and Amy thought she must love Barney more than anything else in the whole world.

"Sit," she said sternly. "And keep guard."

Barney jumped down from the bed but then just rolled over onto his back. His floppy ears spread out onto the pale carpet like a big spill of ink.

"Right," said Amy. "I'm going to check now so you had better be ready, Barney—just in case."

Barney twisted back over onto his tummy and put his nose on the floor near the end of the bed.

"That's better. Ready, steady..."

Amy dived to one side of the bed. Her damp hair trailed onto the carpet and her eyes swept from one end to the other.

"Hurray, Barney—no monsters for you to eat today. Bad luck."

Amy's mum bustled into the room.

"Oh, my goodness, Amy," she said. "What on earth is the dog doing in here? Come here, Barney. Now then, it's time you were going to sleep, young lady. School tomorrow."

Amy heard her dad whistle from downstairs. Barney bounded out and crashed into the door as he went.

"Amy, we've got a big day tomorrow with your Great Aunt arriving."

Amy tried her best to smile. "And Charlotte and Simran are coming as well, don't forget."

"Oh, bother. Yes, I had forgotten. Can't we put them off until another day? It's going to be bad enough with Aunt Scarlet arriving. Goodness knows what trouble will be in store for us when she gets here."

"But why *is* she trouble, Mum?"

Mum closed her eyes and sighed.

"There's always something... I don't know. I just don't know... anyway, Amy you must get into bed—it's getting late. Let's put the light off tonight. You're a big girl now—nearly twelve."

"Sorry, Mum. But you know I would never get to sleep if it was pitch black."

"Well, when Aunt Scarlet has gone, we'll have to sort all this out—being scared of the dark. It's been going on too long. You just need to be brave."

The door clicked shut as Helen went out.

Amy clicked it open again after a minute or so and put her bedside light on. The fringes of the lampshade tickled the back of her hand. She wondered what it must have been like in the old days before electricity and lights. Horrible, she thought. Really horrible.

Her bed was warm, and the white sheets smelled of washing powder. Her pillow was soft and she felt safe.

CHAPTER 3

Strange, Weird Weather

Next morning something felt wrong.

The stillness of the night had been replaced with a strong squally wind. It should have been light, but it was dark. Large drops of rain splattered and drummed against the bedroom window. Amy could hear the sound of the waves from the distant sea. The wind must be whipping the surf into a frenzy because it was rare for Amy to be able to hear it from this distance. Boswell village looked set for a bad storm.

Things were no better inside the house.

Amy arrived at the kitchen to see her mum looking pale and Dad looking worried. Two plates had already somehow been dropped and smashed. Broken china had been brushed into a jumbled pile in a corner. Barney was cowering under the table, his eyes wide and scared.

"Do you think there's going to be a terrible storm?" asked Amy. "It's weird weather isn't it? It's so dark. Not like summer at all."

Helen tried to put a brave face on it.

"You just get your breakfast, love, and then off to school. It will probably have blown over by lunch time."

Amy felt a strange atmosphere in the room as she quickly ate a pile of scrambled egg and a slice of bacon. She looked over at her father and couldn't help but notice his nervous glances.

She frowned.

"Is everything all right, Dad?"

"Yes, yes. Fine, Amy. This stormy weather is just a bit unsettling, that's all—but it's only a bit of wind and rain, isn't it? We can't control it, can we? Wish we could. Please don't go anywhere near the harbour today, Amy. It will be dangerous."

His lips went tight and he was talking to Helen in a low and anxious voice about checking his ancient fishing boat, 'Old Salty', as Amy left the room. She walked into the hall, Barney now following her, and found her school blazer hanging on a hook in amongst the other outdoor stuff on pegs by the front door. She pushed her feet into her shoes, grabbed another coat then bent down and gave Barney a hug. She opened the front door to the roar of wind.

"Have you got your waterproof on, Amy?" Helen shouted.

"Yes, and I've got my scarf and my gloves with me just in case."

Mum was always worrying about her 'catching her death' and getting her blazer and the rest of her school uniform wet. Oh, well, I suppose she has a point, thought Amy. The weather looked awful.

She walked away from the shelter of the row of houses and found herself struggling against a fierce gusting wind. Driving hailstones stung her face as she walked the short distance through Boswell village to the bus stop. She stopped briefly on the old humped stone bridge and looked down at the river. The water looked browner than usual. Must be soil and peat washing down from the moor. The wind was stirring it up. Amy could taste the water as it flecked up. It tasted salty. There was definitely more water than usual washing along—but no wonder. She looked up the valley towards Blackthorn Crag. It looked dark and bleak today, towering above the wet roofs. Amy imagined the steep moor beyond stretching miles and miles without a single person or even a tree. Just endless wet bog. She looked away and her eyes swept to the horizon in the opposite direction. The huge expanse of sea in the distance looked grey and cold. She usually felt comforted by the feeling she had of living in a cosy seaside village but today nothing at all felt cosy or comforting.

Mr Cowley, the school bus driver, grinned when Amy climbed the steps of the bus.

"You look like a drowned rat, lass," he said and thrummed his fingers on the steering wheel. "Looks like a big storm could be brewing. Best get you all to Rushworth as quick as we can."

Amy could never have thought, as she squelched down into her seat behind Simran and Charlotte, that the uneasy conditions outside could have been in any way connected with the arrival of Great Aunt Scarlet. That little old lady...

*

The first lesson of the day was Geography—in a room on its own at the very top of the school. The weather had become ferocious. Their teacher, Mrs Fredrickson, could hardly make herself heard above the sound of the wind whistling round the roof and the clatter of rain and hail against the windows. In the end she told the class to pack up their things. She was moving them to a different room.

Nobody could possibly have predicted what happened next. Amy stood up and was packing away her books and pencils when there was a boom. The window—the huge window near Amy—shook violently and the metal frame began to buckle. The glass shuddered briefly and then it exploded and came crashing into the room.

Everyone started screaming. The glass fractured into

sharp splinters. It pierced into the wood of the desks like daggers. The wind and freezing rain surged in with a sound like an express train through the huge empty hole left in the wall. The room was soaked. Soggy paper swirled up into a raging tornado. Pencils flicked across the room, flew against the walls and skittered across the floor.

"Try to keep calm," Mrs Fredrickson shouted—looking nothing like calm herself.

"Make your way forward. Come on. Let's get out as quickly as we possibly can."

Amy realised that she was bleeding. A shard of glass had sliced into her left arm just below her elbow. Her hand shook. She grabbed her scarf and wrapped it roughly around the wound but, in seconds, dark red was oozing through the thin wool.

Mrs Frederickson was pale. She stood, her body rigid with tension and her hand clutching at the handle of the open door. She quickly shepherded everyone down the stairs until she was the only one left. With a final look at the devastation that had once been a perfectly good solid classroom, she forced the door shut and followed the class down to the lower floor.

*

The first aid member of staff, Miss Driver, made a good job of bandaging Amy's arm. Charlotte and Simran hovered outside the medical room.

"I thought schools were supposed to have windows made of safety glass," said Simran. "That wasn't safety glass, was it—shattering all over us like that?"

"I bet this school is just too old," said Charlotte. "But I bet someone'll get a rocket over it. I can't believe the wind was as strong as that. Weird day and getting weirder."

At the end of school, Simran and Amy walked closely together under an umbrella to the bus stop. The wind had dropped but the rain was getting heavier by the second and thunder rumbled in the distance.

"Will it still be all right to come over to yours tonight what with your arm and everything?" asked Simran.

"Course it will," said Amy. "You and Charlotte can take my mind off it. Please come."

"Ok," said Simran. "See you about seven."

The school bus arrived. Amy trailed her waterproof coat and the unbloodied part of her scarf over the bulge of bandage underneath the sleeve of her blazer so that Mr Cowley wouldn't see it. It would be just like him to draw attention to her with a loud and stupid comment when that was the last thing she wanted. If he did, she thought, everyone on the bus would make a fuss. It was bad enough half the school knowing she had been injured. She couldn't bear the thought of them wanting to look. She didn't even want to talk about it. It was just too awful a day. She couldn't understand why she had been the only one stabbed by the glass—why it had to have been the window right next to her.

The bus slowly wound its way up the steep hill to

Boswell. The river was looking full—dangerously full. It had been raining for more than eight hours. Heavy rain. And the thunder was getting louder.

Lightning ripped across the sky. Huge dark clouds across the moor were looking angry and strange. Amy hardly recognised her village. It seemed to have taken on the look of another place. Another place that was not very nice.

Even though Amy ran as fast as she could with her bag banging against her legs and her arm hurting with the effort, the distance from the bus stop to her front door was far enough for her to arrive with hair dripping in rat's tails and her shoes full of water. She felt as though she couldn't get much wetter and was looking forward to getting into a hot bath despite her arm. She was thinking about how she would keep it dry with a plastic bag when she pushed open the door to the house and nearly fell over.

The hall was full of bags and suitcases.

Oh no. Great Aunt Scarlet. She must have arrived.

CHAPTER 4

Unbelievable

Puddles were forming at Amy's feet on the polished wooden floor of the hall. Barney bounced next to her and jumped up—his claws dug into her leg. Amy gently pushed her little dog away.

The hall suddenly seemed dark. Amy looked up.

The light from the kitchen had been blocked by a person. A very tall woman.

She spoke and her voice was low and unpleasant.

"Don't you dare get water on my luggage, girl. Get away from my cases. And get that wretched animal away too."

Was this Great Aunt Scarlet?

There was no sign of the little old lady in a knitted hat and sensible shoes. In fact, Great Aunt Scarlet's shoes were the complete opposite of sensible. They were unbelievable. High stiletto heels—at least four inches high—shiny and bright red. They were, well, just unbelievable.

Amy tried to take in the spectacle of this woman standing before her. The shoes were only the start. Her legs were covered in black and gold leggings and the slim body was wrapped in a tight snakeskin dress. Her white face was punctured by a smirking mouth smothered in red lipstick. Her hair was black, long and cascading over her shoulders. Even in all the confusion of the moment, Amy couldn't help noticing that she had a thick white streak running through it—just like her own hair.

Amy couldn't speak. She didn't move. The two of them just stared at each other. Amy's skirt dripped into increasingly large puddles. Great Aunt Scarlet narrowed her black eyes and hissed.

"Get away from my cases, girl and that dog. Get it away."

Aunt Scarlet turned. Amy could see her mum looking very nervous.

Scarlet laughed.

"Ha! What on earth have you got here, Helen? Is this the famous Amy? What a sight."

"Oh, Amy," said Helen. "You're soaked. Go straight upstairs and get changed. You're dripping all over Scarlet's bags. Take Barney up with you."

Amy looked up at Great Aunt Scarlet who was grinning, and not in a nice way.

Amy kicked off her shoes and stomped up the stairs, pushing Barney ahead of her. She could hear her mother apologising, grovelling.

"I'm so sorry, Scarlet. So sorry. If there's any damage to your bags, we'll get it sorted out...we'll pay for it to be put right."

Amy couldn't believe what she was hearing. What was her mother thinking of? She must have completely lost her mind.

Barney jumped onto the bed and lay in a black fluffy bundle while Amy peeled off her wet things. She flinched as the sleeve of her shirt caught against the thick bandage and the cut on her arm started to throb. She bunched the clothes into a soggy pile and dropped them next to her bedroom door. She would take them downstairs later and put them into the washer. She put on a pair of jeans and a long-sleeved baggy tee-shirt and then flopped down onto her bed and cuddled up to Barney. She thought with mounting horror about the dreadful woman downstairs. She felt afraid. She started to wonder if this terrible day could somehow have been something to do with her. No, surely not. Could it?

CHAPTER 5

The Horrible Party Trick

Great Aunt Scarlet was upstairs in the spare bedroom when Amy eventually crept downstairs with the wet clothes. She had spent the last half hour listening to poor Dad being ordered about. He had carried all the bags to Scarlet's room and didn't get a single word of thanks.

"Put that one over there, David. That one here. Oh, this is such a tiny wardrobe. No, wait—I've changed my mind—the other bag over here. Be careful, man. Don't damage anything."

Amy wondered why Dad was putting up with it. Why was he letting himself be ordered about like that? He wasn't usually a wimp. It was as if she had some power over him and he wasn't able to stand up to her. It was going to be terrible if the whole visit was going to be as awful as these first few hours. How would they all cope?

Amy pushed her school uniform into the washer and looked over at her mother. She looked pale. She had a cup of tea in her hand and was holding it to her cheek. She stared out of the window—in a world of her own.

"Mum. Are you all right?"

Helen jumped and then she seemed to recover.

"Mum," said Amy. "This woman..." She lowered her voice. "Why have I never met her before if she's my aunt? I can't see how she can be my great aunt. She's far too young. She's nothing like a grandma, is she? Is she Grandma's sister? I don't get it. Anyway, Mum, how long is she staying? She won't still be here when it's my birthday, will she?"

Helen shook her head and looked down.

"She's a mystery. No-one quite knows how old she is. She has been part of the family for as long as I can remember. She never seems to age at all. We haven't seen her since the day you were born, Amy. She arrived to see you but then she just disappeared—until now. And as for how long she's staying, I don't know."

"It's all very weird," Amy said under her breath, and when she looked over at Mum again, she could see tears in her mother's eyes.

It was only then that Helen noticed the lumpy bandage under the tee-shirt sleeve.

"What has happened, Amy? Why didn't you tell me about this straight away? This is awful. Oh, my goodness. I knew things would start to go wrong as soon as..." Her voice trailed off and she bit her lip.

Amy agreed with her mum. Everything did seem wrong. Even her parents seemed to have turned into different people.

The doorbell rang and Amy was relieved to see her two best friends standing on the doorstep.

"Quickly, come in before you get even more soaked. I think the weather is getting worse—so wet, isn't it?" said Amy. "Anyway, come into this mad house." She tried to smile but her mouth just stayed in a thin line.

"How's your arm?" asked Charlotte, bending down to stroke Barney's soft ears. "Does it sting? Wasn't it frightening in Geography? Seems like the whole world's suddenly gone nuts."

"My Great Aunt is here. I'll tell you about her."

They quietly climbed up the stairs with Barney and gently closed the bedroom door.

Amy started whispering to them—about the red shoes, about the snakeskin dress and about how horrible it had all been but—at that moment—the bedroom door crashed open and there stood Great Aunt Scarlet.

She had changed into a pair of sleeveless silky emerald

green pyjamas and purple slippers studded with what looked like diamonds. Her dark hair was knotted up into an untidy pile on the top of her head, kept in place with three golden pins.

Amy gasped silently. She could clearly see a perfectly straight blue line running all the way down Great Aunt Scarlet's right arm and to the tip of her middle finger. Just like her own.

Amy glanced at Charlotte and Simran. Their mouths were hanging open.

Great Aunt Scarlet grinned and then leaned back against the door frame. She closed her eyes for a second and then glared at them.

"So," she said in an icy voice. "Who have we got here? I would have thought you might have devoted this evening to welcoming me into your home, Miss Amy—however, I see you have decided to make other plans."

"But—" started Amy.

"Don't interrupt, girl," Aunt Scarlet barked.

"Well, very nice to meet you two schoolgirls," said Scarlet in a simpering voice.

Charlotte and Simran nodded dumbly and mumbled something about being pleased to meet her.

"I presume these two are your very best friends, Amy," said Aunt Scarlet. "Hmmm."

"Yes," said Amy. "We've grown up together."

"It's a nasty night to be out," Scarlet said. "Very wet— and could get wetter I'll be bound. I can see the river from my window. Seems to be filling up. Hope we don't get a flood, girls. Do you think we might?"

She walked into the room and traced a long fingernail around Neddy-Knock-Knees. She smiled and the red lipstick stretched into a grimace.

Simran and Charlotte glanced awkwardly at each other. Amy spoke up.

"I'm sure the rain will have stopped by the morning, erm, Great Aunty," she said, giving a nervous little laugh. "Can't rain for ever, can it?"

Scarlet stopped smiling.

"Do not call me 'Great Aunt'," she said. "My name is Scarlet. Plain Scarlet. That is how you should address me from now on. Understand?"

Amy nodded.

Scarlet glanced down for a moment and then looked up. Her eyes were different. The white parts had changed to a deep yellow.

She looked over at the neat pile of books and homework on the desk. Amy couldn't stop staring at her. Scarlet's eyes were glowing, brighter and brighter and, in a few seconds, it seemed that light was streaming out of them. She was in a sort of trance.

"Aunty—" Amy started to say. "Scarlet..."

Papers on the desk started to move by themselves and to swirl above the table. Amy clung onto Simran's shoulder.

The books fell to the floor one by one. Thump, thump,

thump. And then the paper fluttered down on top.

Barney whimpered and cowered away into a corner.

"Horrid, horrid dog," said Scarlet.

She turned towards the girls. Her yellow eyes lingered on Charlotte for a moment, then on Simran and then her eyes snapped shut. When they opened again, the yellow glint and the streaming light had gone.

"Just a little party trick of mine," she said. "Just a bit of fun. Ha ha!"

She flounced out of the room and banged the door behind her.

Amy wasn't really sure what happened next. It was all so fast.

Simran and Charlotte looked at each other and then at Amy and, without a word, they opened the bedroom door, walked down the stairs, picked up their coats and went out into the wet night.

Amy stumbled after them, almost falling over Barney who was clattering down the stairs at her feet.

"You don't have to go," she said, her voice pleading. "You've only just got here, please..."

But the girls had already gone. The front door was standing wide open. The outside light made the raindrops glitter and sparkle. Amy stepped out into the wetness— not caring if she got soaked through. What did it matter? What did anything matter?

As thunder rumbled around her, she became vaguely aware of the throb in her arm under the bandage and her eyes filled with tears.

She went up the stairs in a daze.

In a kind of dream, she went back to her room and sat on the edge of her bed for a long time.

She heard the landing clock chime eight o'clock. She stood up, walked across to the window and peeped behind the bedroom curtains. She saw that, at long last, the rain seemed to be easing off.

Well, at least that was something.

She picked up the books and papers from the floor and pushed them into a heap on top of the desk, not bothering to make them neat. What was the point?

She lay down on the bed and stared up at the ceiling. Things couldn't get much worse, she thought.

She was wrong about that.

CHAPTER 6

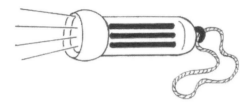

The Wrong Neddy

Scarlet had shut herself into her room. Amy lay on her bed for a long time.

Eventually, she rubbed her red eyes, picked up her nightdress and went into the bathroom.

She locked the door, clicked on the light and looked in the mirror. And then—blackness. The light had gone out and it was as dark as Amy had ever known it.

She groped for the door and heard her father shouting downstairs. The whole house was dark.

Amy shivered on the landing, her pulse starting to pound behind her eyes.

A flickering light appeared downstairs and got closer until the face of her dad appeared like a ghost.

Amy could hardly speak.

"Dad," she whispered. "Whatever..."

"It's okay, Amy," David tried to reassure her. "It's a power cut, that's all, the whole village is out—probably something to do with all this bad weather we're having. Don't worry, they'll be sorting it out at the power station. I bet it'll be on again in a jiffy. Mum and I are just going next door to check on Mrs Judd. We are hoping she's gone to her sisters, but if she hasn't and she's home alone, she'll be in a terrible state. Here, take this torch for now. It's a good one with new batteries. We'll be back as soon as we can."

"But, Dad—"

"Don't make a fuss, Amy. It's bad enough. Just be a brave girl. Get into bed if you like. Mum will come up in a few minutes. The lights will probably have come back on by then. Look, Barney's come to keep you company."

The black, rubbery torch was heavy and far too big in Amy's small hands.

Dad turned. Amy could hear him taking each stair with care.

Amy started to push at her bedroom door. But there was something strange.

There was light under Great Aunt Scarlet's door. Not the wispy flickering light of a torch or a candle but a strong light—a normal light. The lights in Aunt Scarlet's room were on. Barney whined.

Amy started to think she was losing her mind. She closed her bedroom door, tried her light switch with no luck and then slowly made her way over to the bed with the help of the torch. She pulled back the soft covers, clambered in, pulled her knees up to her chest and rested her throbbing arm to one side. It was quiet. Too quiet.

The torch got muddled up in the bed covers. Amy picked it up, balanced it awkwardly with one hand on the top of her knees and then swivelled it round so that it shone over towards her desk. It twinkled briefly in the mirror. Everything looked different in the thin beam of light. The chair cast a monstrous shadow on the wall.

Amy tried hard to remember what to do in these scary moments. She hugged Barney and stroked his soft fur. She began to say her nine times table. And then she hummed one of the tunes Mum used to sing to her when she was a little girl.

She tried to remember what it was like to be small. She remembered party cakes and balloons and trips to the park, playing on swings and throwing a frisbee with Mum and Grandma on the beach. She remembered all the fishing trips with Dad in his boat, 'Old Salty'. Such happy times.

She remembered buying the Neddy-Knock-Knees picture and Mum fixing it onto her wardrobe. Little Neddy-Knock-Knees.

Amy twisted the torch away from the desk and towards the wardrobe. If I look at Neddy-Knock-Knees, she thought, maybe I will feel brave and calm.

The light travelled from the bottom of the wardrobe door to the familiar place near the top where Neddy-Knock-Knees would be looking over at her with those big, kind eyes and that sweet little face.

Amy gasped at what she saw. Barney let out a high whine. Neddy-Knock-Knees had gone.

In his place was a monstrous face with flared nostrils and red slits for eyes. The ears were laid flat across the head and the coat was a mass of dark wet matted fur. Behind him, the trees were bare, black and spiky. Terrifying faces peered out and yellow googly eyes blinked and winked from between the branches.

But wait—the creature—it *was* Neddy-Knock-Knees.

Neddy-Knock-Knees had changed into this hideous beast. Staring. Staring straight at Amy. And his mouth— his mouth was moving. Long grey teeth leered at her, dribbles of foaming saliva collected at the corners of his snarling lips.

Amy couldn't breathe. Her heart was galloping, her hands felt numb.

Without warning, the lights came on.

Amy's hand still gripped the torch—its tiny light looking pathetic now in the brightness of the room. She clicked it off but didn't let go.

She looked at the wardrobe. There was Neddy-Knock-

Knees.

His big brown doleful eyes with the beautiful eyelashes looked at her. His sweet nose, his little spotted coat. Everything was the same as it had always been.

Amy heard laughing. High pitched. It didn't stop. The laughing went on and on and on. Great Aunt Scarlet was laughing until her lungs might burst.

CHAPTER 7

Alone

*A*my didn't really go to sleep that night. Images of the bad Neddy on the wardrobe filled her head and her body shook. Perhaps she was going mad.

Next morning, Amy struggled out of bed. Her eyes felt sore and her head was aching. Maybe she was ill. Maybe she had a temperature. Maybe the terrors of last night were the hallucinations of a girl who was getting ill.

*

Amy heard noises outside her window. She quickly pulled back the curtains and saw a group of people from the village standing in a huddle. A dog was barking in the distance. The people looked worried. It was raining again.

She got dressed, making sure to be careful to pull her sleeve gently over her bad arm. She crept downstairs and grabbed a bite of breakfast even though she didn't feel at all like having any. Scarlet had not appeared yet, thank goodness. Mum and Dad were nowhere to be seen.

Amy was hopeful that when she got to the bus, she could talk the whole thing over with Charlotte and Simran. They would be able to help. It would just be nice to talk about it.

The river looked very different. Not gentle, quiet and babbling as usual—but huge and raging. Amy didn't stop for long on the bridge but hurried on to the bus stop. Everywhere smelled of wet soil and leaves. She tried hard not to get too wet because Mr Cowley was bound to make a comment again, trying to be funny.

But even Mr Cowley did not seem to be himself this morning. He looked serious for once and he also looked as though he hadn't slept. Simran and Charlotte were not on the bus. They must have got a lift today from Charlotte's dad.

Mr Cowley looked up at Amy but didn't speak. He just nodded curtly, crunched the bus into gear and pulled out onto the hill. Amy sat down and tried to look out through the filth on the window. Rain was streaking through the dirt. It made snaking streams as it slithered across the glass.

Amy pressed her fingers against the bandage on her arm. She would ask Miss Driver to look at it again today and see if it was any better or if it needed a new dressing to keep it clean and dry. She didn't think it could be much better. It still hurt like mad when she touched it.

More and more wet people climbed aboard and eventually the big bus wheels swished around the last corner. The brakes hissed and the bus parked up in the school grounds. Amy could see Simran at the end of the bus shelter. Good—she was waiting for her. She needed to apologise for last night and to Charlotte too for the disgraceful behaviour of her Great Aunt. She hoped they would understand. Maybe they would be able to help her to think of a way of getting the woman out of her home and things could get back to normal.

Amy climbed down the steps of the bus and ran along to her friend.

Something was wrong.

Charlotte was coming across the narrow road leading into the school. Her black shoes shone with wetness. She didn't look at Amy but came straight across to Simran and they linked arms.

And then they both turned and glared at Amy. They narrowed their eyes. Was it a trick of the light or were the whites of their eyes pink, maybe even red?

"Hi," said Amy, hesitating. "Everything okay?"

They didn't speak and continued to glare. Then, they started laughing—a horrible mean laugh—and turned their backs on her.

Amy closed her eyes, trying hard to prevent tears. She took a deep breath and walked into school to her first lesson—science with Mr Carr. She had been hoping that her project about the water cycle would get a good mark. She had enjoyed learning about the way water dries up from the surface of the earth and becomes invisible until it reappears again as clouds.

Clouds, she thought. White fluffy clouds. But, now out of the window, all she could see were low black clouds, becoming lower and darker by the minute and spilling rain in torrents. Somehow, any interesting science about the water cycle didn't matter. Nothing seemed important anymore.

Amy sat on her own, her heart beating fast and her stomach in a knot of fear.

Mr Carr walked into the room. There was something not right. Amy noticed that he didn't look at all as he normally did. He was usually dressed smartly and ready to teach science with a smile on his face and an experiment set up on his table at the front of the classroom.

Amy felt even more fearful. She ran her hand along the rough edge of the wooden bench.

Mr Carr stared at Amy. His clothes and his hair were dishevelled. His eyes looked wild—the whites of his eyes were pink. They were definitely pink, maybe even red.

"How dare you hand in work like this to me, Amy Harrington," he barked. Amy felt her knee start to tremble.

The project landed with a thump next to her. She could see the drawings she had done of the water cycle with the carefully coloured diagrams and neat labels.

The class fell silent.

Amy bit her lip until she could taste blood. Mr Carr curled his hand into a fist and banged it down onto the bench.

"Grade F!" he said, his voice cracking. "It's rubbish. A disgrace."

Mr Carr's eyes became even more wild and staring, his cheeks almost purple. Bits of spit came onto his lips as he spoke. He leaned over and he smelled of smoke and sweat and stale coffee.

Amy felt as though she might faint. Her eyes misted over and her head pounded. Mr Carr turned away, walked the length of the room to his computer and sat with his back to the class. Everyone looked at each other but mostly they looked at Amy. Some laughed quietly but they also looked scared and when the bell went at last, they bundled out of the classroom in relief.

Amy heard Charlotte and Simran whispering and giggling.

"He must be having a stupid nervous breakdown or something," said Charlotte. "He looked weird."

Amy walked slowly out of the classroom and sat alone on a wooden bench in the corridor.

She watched Simran run towards her and, for a second, she felt hopeful. But Simran just ran past, ignoring her and yelled to a group of others further down the corridor.

"Mr Carr is going home," she shouted. "Mrs Fletcher was helping him get into her car. He looked really awful. He could hardly walk. The wind nearly blew him over and he must have been crying because his eyes had turned red."

Amy couldn't get the image out of her mind. Mr Carr. One of the very best teachers at Rushworth. Lovely Mr Carr with red eyes and a purple face. Amy looked down at her work. Grade F.

Her work was excellent. She knew that. It was the same as always. Grade A. Her eyes filled with tears. She angrily blinked them away, stood up and walked outside, pulling up her hood against the driving rain.

Charlotte and Simran were running in front of her with the rest of the class as they made their way across the school campus towards the technical subjects block.

A huge lake had formed in a dip at one side of the narrow road just beyond where the bus normally parked. Rain was splattering into it. Simran and Charlotte stood at the edge of the water with linked arms. Simran grinned over at Amy but her dark pink eyes looked unkind and were narrowed.

Amy smiled back, uncertain, her lips pressed together.

Charlotte stamped hard in the lake of water and then she scraped the heel of her shoe through the thick layer of gravel at the bottom of the pool and swept a wave of dark muddy water high into the air. The muck hit Amy hard and cold. Streaks of black filth covered her face and before she was aware of it, her arms had been grabbed. Simran dug her fingers into the wound on Amy's arm. Amy screamed and tried to pull away, but she was dragged by both girls roughly towards the lake. They pushed her hard and suddenly she was on her knees. The bottom of her skirt quickly soaked up the filthy freezing water. Her bag sank in front of her.

She looked up, eyes wide. Tears burned onto her face and her voice choked into a muffled sob.

The girls were heading towards the school entrance. They turned to watch Amy struggle to her feet and lift the dripping bag from the water.

Two boys walked past and stared.

"Bit clumsy," one said.

"Idiot must have decided to have a swim." They laughed at their own jokes and neither of them made any effort to help her.

In the far distance, a group of teachers came out of the glass entrance doors and spoke to some of the pupils.

Amy saw a boy dance and then jump into the air with a whoop.

The group turned and started to walk away from the building. "School's closed," came a shout. "The boiler room's flooded."

Amy couldn't think straight. She knew she just wanted

to get home and out of these wet clothes. She wanted to go back to bed, to be asleep and for this terrible nightmare to end.

CHAPTER 8

The Flood

*A*my began the steep mile long walk up the hill towards her village. The rain had eased to a drizzle now. Cold black sludge dripped from the edge of her skirt and down the back of her legs. She dangled her soaking bag at arm's length. She didn't want to think about all the books and the work that would be ruined inside. Her bad arm throbbed.

She finally reached the first houses of the village. She saw that the river had burst its banks and the water was moving fast, freely and noisily—flattening the grass on the riverbank. All the blades of grass were being pulled along in one flowing direction. It looked like a soft shiny green carpet.

She started to run towards the bridge. The brown water, not too far below, was boiling and churning in a loud and angry torrent. It looked like a huge and terrible writhing snake.

Amy was nearly at her house when she heard a crash. She looked up in horror to see that a screaming waterfall had formed and was pouring a deluge of muddy water, foam and rocks over the edge of Blackthorn Crag where no waterfall had been before. It joined another torrent that was now pulsing hard and fast—forcing its way through the narrow valley entrance at the top of the village leading down from the Moor.

Amy jumped up onto Mrs Judd's garden wall just in time. The flood swept past less than a few metres away. The water surged forward. It picked up a motorcycle and sent it careering along in the frantic waves until it clattered against a house wall opposite. She heard children screaming in the distance and men shouting. She scrambled across the overgrown garden to the wall of her own house, scraping her knee on the rough stones and half falling onto the soil and plants at the edge of her father's neat lawn. She could hear Barney barking and her mother's muffled cries from inside the house. She picked herself up, stumbled across to the back door and fell heavily against the brown wood. Then she banged with her fist until her hand was full of pain.

The door jerked open. Amy stumbled in and fell onto the hard, grey tiles of the kitchen. Her soaking bag slithered forward. The legs of a chair screeched against the floor when the bag hit.

Helen was standing above her, breathing fast. Her eyes wide.

"We've got to get out, Mum," Amy shouted. "The water. It's going to be a massive flood. Where's Dad?"

Helen didn't move.

"Mum," Amy shrieked. "Mum."

Her mother stood, rigid—her mouth open in a silent scream.

Amy knew she had to do it. She slapped Helen across the face. Her mother jolted and breathed in with a loud gasp.

There was no time.

"Where's Dad?"

"Out," Mum said, her voice quiet and trembling. "He and Scarlet. Went to Penkeridge."

"Right. Good. Come on, Mum—we've got to escape—there's a disaster happening outside."

She dragged her mother by the arm to the front of the house and shouted desperately for Barney to come.

Black stinking water was already pouring under and around the sides of the door. It was lapping up to the bottom of the window. Huge tree branches swirled about in the torrent outside and then danced away, off down the hill. A red car bobbed past the window. It was upside down.

Amy could hear Barney barking and whining upstairs.

"It's no good, Mum. We can't get out. We'll have to get upstairs. Come on."

Amy glanced down to see the pattern on the carpet disappearing—submerging under a wave of disgusting brown sludge. Amy pushed her mother onto the first stair, then jumped down with a loud splash and slopped across the living room. She picked up Helen's phone.

The wooden window started to let in water around the edges. It sprayed in, screaming and hissing as it came. Jets of water were forcing their way in.

Her mother was shouting. "Amy, Amy, come on."

"I'm here, Mum. I'm right behind you."

Amy banged three nines on the phone. She was told by a ridiculously calm woman that the emergency vehicles were already on their way.

"Get as high as you can," the woman said. "Don't worry about any possessions—keep yourselves as far away from the water as possible."

From the bedroom, the spectacle outside was like a scene from hell.

The water had already risen halfway up the house. The stench from downstairs was terrible. Amy's mother had stopped her panic and a calmness came over her.

"Pull the loft ladder down, Amy," she said, her voice

strong. "We might need to get up into the roof."

"What about poor Mrs Judd?" gasped Amy.

"Not at home," her mother said, her voice now breaking and trembling. "She's at her sister's. Th...thank goodness she has not had to see all this horror."

Amy reached forward and grabbed Barney by his collar. He was cowering against Amy's bedroom door.

"We're getting the worst of it," said Mum looking out of the landing window, her face distraught and a sob in her voice. "The water's mostly missing the other houses— look."

The wall of filth was bouncing around Mrs Judd's garden before striking hard against Amy's house and then veering abruptly away down towards the centre of the village. It was following the course of what was once the gentle river, but it now surged across the car park and on down towards the school. Cars were being picked up and tossed about like toys. They joined the thunderous raging turmoil of uprooted trees and other debris forging and barging its way down the hill.

They heard a crash downstairs and the house shuddered.

"That's it, Amy. We must get into the roof."

Amy pushed Barney in front of her up the thin cold rungs of the rickety loft ladder. The ladder creaked. Barney's body was shaking. He whined and resisted Amy's efforts to push him up. At last she grunted and used her shoulder and all her strength to force him through the small hole in the ceiling. Then she reached back down for Helen's hand.

Mum's voice was strong.

"I'm all right," she said. "I'm coming easily behind you. Let's get up and safe."

The house shuddered again. Amy could hear the loud sound of water from below. The downstairs window must have caved in.

Once they were up, Helen pushed the trapdoor cover back in place and clicked on the light.

Everything was suddenly quiet and eerily calm. Barney had got himself into a corner at the far end under the eaves and was still trembling and whining.

"It's okay, Barney," said Amy. "We'll be all right. You'll see. Come here, boy. Come over here with us. Please."

Barney looked over at her with frightened eyes. He wouldn't come.

Amy sank down next to her mother. The bandage on her arm had become loose and started to unravel. Her squelching shoes were covered in stinking muck, her socks were soaked, and her legs covered in filth. Her skirt was ripped, and her knee was badly grazed and bleeding.

She began to hurt all over.

Helen was speaking into the phone. "Number 32, Main Street," she was saying, trying to stop the panic showing on her face from affecting her voice. "Yes, we're in the roof. Downstairs is flooded...the window out maybe we think... yes...safe so far...two of us...me and my daughter and our dog...yes, all safe so far...thank you...yes, we'll wait." Her breath was coming in frightened bursts. "Of course, we'll wait."

Despite the terrible situation they were faced with, Amy almost smiled. Well, what else could they do but wait to be rescued. Swim for it? Fly away like a bird?

Amy rested her head on Mum's lap. Helen started humming and swaying back and forth. Then the humming turned to singing—one of the songs she used to sing when Amy was little. One of the songs she used to sing around the time they had put up the picture of Neddy-Knock-Knees on the wardrobe door—the time when everything was safe and normal. Those normal times. Just at this moment they felt very far away.

Amy sat up and looked around. The loft was full of boxes and bags. A dusty heap of dark blankets were piled up in one corner and some Christmas decorations sparkled out of a box near the hatch. Amy pulled one of the boxes towards her. A photograph album lay near the top.

"Look at these old photos, Mum," she said. "Is that you when you were a little girl? Is the other girl your friend?" Amy stared intently at the girl. "But Mum," she said. "She...she's a bit like me, isn't she—look she's even got a white streak in her hair. Who is she?"

Helen looked at the photograph and flicked through the album. There were more lots more pictures of the young girl with the white streak and there were more as she got a bit older. She was often with Mum and Grandma in the pictures.

"I don't know who she is," said Helen. "I feel as though I should know who she is. She seems familiar. But I just can't think, Amy. I don't know who she is."

The sound was faint at first but there was no doubt—a helicopter. The sound was getting louder.

Helen put the album back in the box and started singing again. The sound of the helicopter drowned out her voice. Suddenly there was a shudder and a rumbling. The light went out and the darkness seemed complete. The noises outside were muffled. It was dark and warm.

And then suddenly, it was noisy and bright and cold.

The end of the house had broken away and taken most of the roof with it.

The helicopter hovered directly above, and all hell seemed to have broken loose.

Barney was only inches from the cracked floor and a drop down into the swirling mass of raging water below. He had almost been swept down with the rubble and the heap of jumble and boxes near to him, but he had somehow managed to scramble up onto a thick joist of wood. The downdraft from the helicopter was forcing his ears into a ridiculous wobbly dance.

Amy screamed. "Barney, please don't fall. I'm coming...I'm coming to get you."

A voice boomed through a megaphone from the helicopter.

"Please stay exactly where you are—we're sending a man down to bring you out. Well done. We'll have you safe in a couple of minutes. Well done."

Helen put her hand on Amy's good arm.

"I'm so sorry, love," she yelled above the noise of the whirling blades. "We're going to have to leave Barney behind. We can't risk it. It's too dangerous."

Amy looked over at her little dog. He was shaking—his eyes pleading and terrified.

Amy shook Mum's hand off and stood up.

The wind from the helicopter made her topple forward. She fell onto her stomach and began to inch her way over towards Barney.

Helen was screaming her name.

A pair of thick yellow boots landed next to them. The voice was loud and fierce.

"Don't even think of it...what's the girl's name?" he asked Helen.

"It's my daughter. Her name is Amy."

"Don't even think of it, Amy," he said in a still loud but gentler voice. "The floor could give way at any moment."

The man tried to grab her arm. Her bad arm.

Amy struggled and pushed him off then lurched quickly away from him to where Barney was sitting and shivering on the thick roof beam. The wind from the helicopter was almost overwhelming and the noise deafening.

"Right," shouted the man. "I'll have to take you first,

Mum. No arguments."

Helen was crying now. She looked across at Amy and Barney and then dropped her head and meekly let the man fasten the hoist round her. She coiled away with him into the air and out of sight.

Amy hugged Barney. They were on the edge of nothingness and a boiling cauldron of water buffeted what was left of the house. Any minute...any minute now...

The man was back. The yellow boots stood solid—next to her.

He took an orange bag from his jacket, grabbed Barney by the collar and quickly bundled him into the bright cloth. He secured Amy in the straps and then the three of them twirled round and round, up towards the roaring of the waiting helicopter.

*

Amy's hair was flung about and swirled madly in the wind. It felt very cold. She could see as they were spinning, that more helicopters were hovering nearby and a huge number of emergency vehicles with their lights flashing, were a little way up the hillside.

Towards the bottom of the hill, she could see tall waves of black water as it tumbled and crashed noisily downwards. At the side lay heaps of mud, cars and bicycles pushed together in a tangled mess. On the hill sides, people were running in panic or standing together in groups, their faces showing the same shocked expression, watching the terrible scene unfold.

CHAPTER 9

Safe

It was chaos in the village hall. People were running in with blankets and sandwiches and flasks of hot tea. More rescued people were being brought in. Mr Armitage, the church warden, had taken it upon himself to make a note of all the names, times of arrival and other details.

"Is there anyone you want to contact, Helen?" said Mr Armitage. "Was David in the house with you?"

Amy sat on a blanket spread out on the dusty hall floor. Her back rested against the wall. Susan, the nurse from the doctors, had attended to her the moment she had arrived—cleaned her with a soft cloth and warm water, bandaged up her knee and her arm and given her some sweet tea in a thick blue mug.

Helen thanked Mr Armitage and then started talking to David on a borrowed phone, half crying. "Yes...it has been terrible...terrifying. No—it...it's all right...Amy is safe...I'm safe...even Barney is with us...yes, if you could get here...as soon as...no, I don't think the house will have survived...maybe completely washed away...heaven knows... but the main thing is that we are all safe." She cried harder now. "Please get here as soon as you can, David."

CHAPTER 10

The Change

Mr and Mrs Craythorpe, friends in the village, were very kind in finding rooms in their house for them all, even Scarlet. Barney was welcomed too.

Their home, Beech Lodge, stood at the very top of the hill overlooking Boswell village. Mrs Craythorpe told them how she had watched the disaster of the flood from an upstairs window. She said she had hardly been able to breathe when she saw Helen and Amy being rescued. She had thought it absolutely incredible that David and Scarlet had been out of the village and had escaped just by chance.

She had vowed to help them all in whatever way she could.

Beech Lodge was a very large house—probably the largest house in the village. Amy had her own room just down the corridor from her parents. Scarlet's room was far away, on the other side of the house where she mostly kept herself to herself and Amy was pleased not to have too much to do with her. She was hoping that soon, her visit would be over and that once their house was repaired— once this strange aunt had left—maybe things could get back to normal.

Two weeks after the flood, Scarlet was still with them. Amy just couldn't get to grips with the big change in Great Aunt Scarlet. No—she must remember to call her 'Scarlet' and leave out the 'Great Aunt' part. No point in upsetting her again.

Scarlet appeared to be as upset and as concerned about the family as any normal person would be. Any normal adult.

On the day of the flood, Scarlet had sat down straight away next to Amy on the floor of the village hall. Amy hardly recognised her. She had changed her hairstyle. The black hair was now pulled back into a neat bun and she wore a pair of dark brown rimmed spectacles. The thick streak of white hair on the side of Scarlet's head was almost hidden.

Scarlet's voice seemed to have changed too from what Amy had remembered. It was now gentle and caring. She called Amy the bravest person she had ever met.

"How wonderful that you saved dear little Barney," she said. "You are such a good girl. So brave—so very brave." Her eyes glinted as she spoke. "We must make sure that you get an extra special surprise for your birthday, I know your birthday is soon, isn't it?"

Amy looked at Scarlet. She now seemed a good woman, kind and affectionate. Amy hoped that maybe she was going to like this new version of Scarlet. And her birthday wasn't far away now. It made her feel excited.

CHAPTER 11

The Offer

The massive village clean-up operation had gone into full swing as soon as the flood waters had gone down. Everyone in the district had worked hard and lent a hand in one way or another. It was still very smelly though. There was a lot of damage, but the amazing thing was that not one single person had been killed or seriously injured. People said it was a miracle. Amy worried that maybe a cat or a dog might have been drowned but the facts were as plain as plain. Nothing was found dead—not even an ant.

"It's just as well the school was evacuated," said Helen. "Part of it has collapsed and the ground floor is four feet deep in stinking mud. You won't be going back there for a while, Amy. They'll have to find somewhere else for you all. Maybe Parklands School will be able to take you. Have you heard from Charlotte and Simran to find out what their plans are?"

Amy had decided not to say anything to Mum about the incident with Charlotte and Simran on the morning of the flood. So many strange things had happened. Amy was beginning to wonder whether she had dreamt the whole thing. But as the days went by without a single contact— even though she had tried desperately to make sure they were all right—she knew that something had gone terribly wrong and that was the thing that worried her more than anything else.

When Amy first saw what was left of her home, she was shocked. She had been born there. Her whole life was wrapped up in the house. She and her friends had played for hours in the garden and her bedroom and now...

In fact—her own bedroom and the spare room had only just survived, but Mum and Dad's room had completely disappeared and there was nothing at all left downstairs that had been untouched by the disgusting mud. Helen had cried when she realised that her big box of photographs had been ruined. Some of them had washed away.

Workers and emergency people were brought in.

They put up tall metal props to keep safe what was left of the house, but it was in a terrible state. Helen said they wouldn't be able to return to it for months.

"But where will we live?" asked Amy. "Are we going to stay for ages with the Craythorpes?"

Amy noticed the brief furtive glance between Mum and Dad, but it wasn't until later that evening that they called her into the Craythorpes' living room so that they could speak to her properly.

Amy perched on the edge of one of the huge armchairs, her arm draped around Barney's neck, his soft ear under her hand.

Helen looked calm, maybe a little nervous—but David looked upbeat. Scarlet was sitting in a distant corner of the room. She was quiet—like a little mouse.

Dad was first to speak.

"Now then, Amy," he began in an overly cheerful voice.

Amy felt scared. She thought she might be sick. What on earth was Dad going to say?

"Scarlet has made us a very kind offer."

Mum looked down but didn't say anything.

Amy glanced over at Scarlet who smiled back, a look of total innocence on her face behind those brown spectacles.

Dad continued.

"Since your school has been devastated, Amy, Scarlet has managed to find a place for you at Halewood private school near her home. It's very well-known indeed for excellent results. Many distinguished people have attended."

Dad was rambling on. Amy couldn't believe what she was hearing. He kept going.

"We know you could have gone to Parklands, but Mum and I have discussed it and the plan is for Scarlet to take you to Yorkshire on Monday to settle in. Halewood sounds like a first-rate school. It's a wonderful opportunity, Amy, don't you think?"

Amy could feel a silent scream starting to build up inside her. She hugged Barney closer to her. She looked at her mother. Her mum would not make eye contact.

"But—" she began but then stopped as her dad stood up, walked quickly across to the window and turned back to look at his daughter with a stern look on his face.

"Now, Amy. This is a very generous offer. To go to a school of such excellence would be a dream for most young girls. It will be fantastic for you. Maybe the flood has done us a favour."

Amy could feel her heartbeat pounding in her ears. She looked pleadingly at her mother—her eyes wide with terror.

Mum forced a ridiculous smile.

"But, Mum, what about my birthday? I won't be here for my birthday. I don't want to—"

"We must be grateful to Scarlet," Helen interrupted. "Dad and I have decided to rent a tiny one-bedroom cottage in Yarlsfield village until our house is fixed up. It's already decided, Amy. You and Scarlet will be on the train to North Yorkshire on Monday. It's all booked and paid for. Good girl. Please say thank you to her."

Tears started stinging into Amy's eyes. She tried to fight them back. The scar on her arm began to throb.

She knew that Mum and Dad were doing what they thought was best for her, but she also somehow knew in her heart that the disaster of the flood was only the beginning. In fact, it was probably nothing to what was in store for her. Nothing at all.

Amy looked over at Scarlet. The innocent smile had gone and had been replaced with the smug look of someone who had just won an argument.

She sat up straight but remained in the corner of the room.

"Of course, you will stay with me," she said in a simpering voice. "It will be wonderful for me to get to know you better. We surely have a lot in common."

Scarlet stretched out the fingers of her right hand into the small circle of light under a lamp on the table next to her and there it was—a definite blue line running across to the end of her middle finger, pulsing. She looked directly at Amy and raised her eyebrows. A few strands of black hair then inexplicably loosened themselves from Scarlet's neat bun and curled around her face. Amy couldn't be absolutely certain as Scarlet stared at her, but her eyes had turned a strange yellow colour. A very strange yellow colour. Maybe it was just a trick of the light or the spectacles. But Amy didn't think so.

*

That night Amy couldn't sleep. Her future had been decided and there was nothing she could do. Her parents had made a decision. She still couldn't believe why they could possibly have agreed to it but, as things stood, she now had absolutely no choice but to go with it. Barney was curled up at the bottom of her bed. He opened one eye as she crept past him on her way to the bathroom.

She clicked on the light and her reflection in the mirror lit up. The streak of white in her hair was glowing. It was much brighter than usual. She thought of the young girl's similar hair in her mother's photographs. She thought of the white streak in Scarlet's hair. Why was the streak in her own hair shimmering and shining tonight? Why?

The blue line down her arm was tingling with an electrical pulse. Amy wondered if the girl in the photograph had a blue line down her arm. Who was that girl and where was she now? Could there be some link between the girl and Scarlet and herself? Amy shivered at the thought. If there was a link, it felt scary. There was no way that she wanted to have anything in common with Scarlet. It was the last thing on earth that she could have wished for.

CHAPTER 12

Trying to be Brave

Next morning, Amy walked slowly down the hill towards the village. Barney was barking and bouncing along next to her. Her eyes swept across the cottages and houses of Boswell. Even now, weeks after the flood, everywhere seemed nothing but full of mess and destruction.

The stink of mud was horrible. The reports had said that over 50,000 tonnes of water had poured through the village over a few hours and that, amongst it, tons of sewerage had been washed into the flood. No wonder there was still a terrible smell and why the people clearing up had been dressed in orange suits and wearing thick gloves and face masks.

The little humped back bridge that Amy had crossed every morning had disappeared apart from a few large chunks of stone embedded into the mud. In its place was a new bright metal structure secured to the banks of the river with thick wire cables and square anchors which had been forced into the ground.

Amy bent down and pushed her fingers into Barney's soft fur. She looked over at the temporary bridge. A man and a woman were halfway across and looking up the valley. Amy walked towards them. She put one hand on the cold metal railing and ran her fingers across the smooth raised rivets. She looked down to the water. The river was nothing more now than a pathetic trickle. Deep raw gouges of smelly bright yellow mud stood at either side. A few stray branches were wedged across the gap.

"Hello, Amy," said the woman.

Amy recognised her from the craft shop in the village. She was someone Mum sometimes used to chat to.

"How are you?" asked the woman. "We heard about your dramatic rescue. We are sorry to see your house has been so badly damaged—but you and your Mum were lucky to escape, weren't you? The flood has been such a terrible shock for all of us."

Amy pulled her lips together and nodded. "We are hoping our house will soon be fixed up and yes, the rescue people were amazing."

The woman's husband leaned forward and rubbed the top of Barney's head.

"The school's a mess," he said. "Some are saying it will have to be re-built—maybe even moved to a new site altogether. Are you starting at Parklands with the others next week?"

Amy was quiet for a moment and then smiled and spoke in a loud and confident voice.

"Actually, I've been invited to join a private school for a while," she said. "It's near my aunt's. We're leaving on Monday for Yorkshire."

"Private school, eh?" said the woman, pulling down the corners of her mouth.

"Yorkshire, eh," said her husband with a snort. "I've heard it can be a bit draughty up that end of the world. Don't forget to pack a vest, will you."

CHAPTER 13

Explosion

Monday arrived.

"All packed then?" asked Dad, trying far too hard to be upbeat and cheerful. He ran his hands through his hair, giving away his nervousness.

Amy tried her best not to make it worse for him.

"Mum and I have got everything in the case and bags that we can think of," she said.

"Good, good," said Dad. "Are you excited?"

"Erm..." Amy began.

Amy's mum flustered into the room, looking hot.

"Scarlet is just about ready," she said. "I can't believe that every single one of her bags managed to escape damage in the flood. It's a miracle, isn't it?"

"I'll take this big case down then," said Dad. He heaved it off the bed, crashed out of the door and then clattered with unnecessary speed down the stairs until it landed with a loud bang on the tiled hall floor of Beech Lodge.

Amy flopped down onto the bed. Barney jumped up next to her and licked her face. She was going to miss him so much.

"Mum," she said. "I don't think I can do this. I can't. I don't want to—how will I manage at night—in the dark? I'll be so scared. I want to be here at home with you. I want to be at home for my birthday."

Helen's hand shook a little.

"I think you'll be fine, Amy. I expect Scarlet will have a lovely room ready for you. It will be an adventure and she will help you celebrate your birthday."

Mum's eyes gave her away. She looked worried and upset.

Amy swept her hand across her smooth pillow.

"What if I don't get on with anyone at the new school? What if they don't like me?"

"Of course they'll like you," said Mum. "Goodness, Amy. You've had lots of friends ever since you were a little girl. You've always been popular. I bet it will be no time at all before Simran and Charlotte come to visit you. Dad and I will be coming in a couple of weeks."

Amy looked at Mum.

"About Simran and Char—" she started to say, but there was a shout from downstairs. It was Dad.

"We'd better get going, Amy. Taxi will be here in a minute."

"Will you come to the station, Mum?" Amy asked.

Mum started bustling again.

"Best not," she said. "Dad and I will wave you and Scarlet off from here. I said we'd be here when the Craythorpes get back from work. They haven't left us a key. Anyway, you can phone us as soon as you get to Scarlet's to tell us all about the journey."

Mum put her arm around Amy's waist and hugged her. Amy could smell her Mum smell—a combination of soap and hairspray and, well goodness knows. She just smelled of Mum.

Amy looked past Mum's shoulder to the big bedroom window of Beech Lodge. She thought about her own little room, about her little pink wardrobe and about Neddy-Knock-Knees. She hoped he wasn't lonely and that he was his lovely usual self. She would miss him, but he would take care of the bedroom until she came back. Which would be very, very soon, she decided. She looked into her mum's face.

"Mum, you will look after Barney, won't you—until I get back—and Mum—"

Mum nodded but then put her hands up in a 'that's the end of the matter' sort of way. Her eyes were bright and a bit watery.

*

The taxi driver was a short round man with a tattoo on one arm. He was loading Scarlet's bags into the boot of a black and white car. He wasn't having an easy time of it.

"For goodness sake, man, show some respect," Scarlet was snapping. "I would have been better off doing it myself instead of having to watch you flinging things about, you half-wit."

Scarlet flapped around the car, her high heels clicking and her long black hair blowing out behind her in the breeze.

The taxi driver put his hands on his hips.

"Look here, Miss fuss-pot," he said, his face reddening. "You're lucky I've even bothered to get out to give you a hand. I'm a driver—not a bloomin' porter. Sort your own cases out, Missy. I'm getting back in the car."

Scarlet's eyes locked onto the driver's and narrowed.

Amy couldn't help but smile a little. David lifted the cases with care until they were all stacked in the car. He finally slammed the boot with a thud.

"Bye then, Scarlet," he said, shaking her limp hand. "Thanks for this. It's really good of you to have found a place for Amy for this short time. Thanks."

Scarlet held Mum by the shoulders. She closed her eyes and managed nothing more than an overly dramatic air kiss.

"Goodbye, Helen," she said, and then folded herself

neatly into the back of the taxi.

Amy was suddenly wrapped up in her parents' arms.

"As soon as the house is fixed then..." Mum began.

Scarlet opened the car door.

"No time for all that now, Helen," she said. "Get in, Amy. Come on—hurry up."

And before she knew it, Amy was in the car, clutching her little blue school bag and they were on their way. She twisted round to wave. Mum had her hand to her mouth and Dad was holding one arm high in the air until the car went down the hill and around a bend on Church Lane and they disappeared.

Scarlet leaned forward to speak to the driver.

"This car has got a very unpleasant smell," she said.

The driver didn't speak. Amy saw the muscles in his left arm tighten and something twitched in his cheek.

Scarlet waited for a response and, when she didn't get one, she flounced back and pressed her lips together in an angry scowl.

After a journey through the countryside, they arrived into Exeter and the taxi pulled into the front of the station. The driver jumped out, opened the boot and then gestured for Scarlet and Amy to sort out the cases by themselves. Amy pulled the heavy bags and suitcases from the car and piled them up in a jumbled heap on the path. Scarlet didn't help. She merely stared in the direction of the car park exit—a smile playing on her lips. She walked round to the front of the car. The thick tattooed arm was resting on the open window.

"How much?" she said through a mouth that hardly opened.

"It's paid for already," the driver said curtly, nodding towards Amy. "This young girl's father."

He waved a twenty-pound note at her and grinned. Then, he started the car, revved the engine and drove away quickly towards the exit.

Scarlet watched—the strange smile back on her face.

Amy had never before heard such a shocking sound as a car tyre bursting. It was so loud that she jumped backwards with a gasp. Her ears started to buzz. It was like a million balloons bursting all at once and a horrible smell of rubber filled the air.

Scarlet briefly clapped her hands together, closed her eyes and nodded. Then, with a sniff, she turned away and strode towards the station to find someone to bring out a trolley for the bags.

CHAPTER 14

Witch

The train was late. Announcements kept them updated about a hold up on the line. Scarlet and Amy sat on a comfortable metal seat, newly painted in silver and green.

The station was quite a pretty one. Troughs of bright flowers were dotted about. Groups of hanging baskets hung from the ornate ceiling. Red and yellow nasturtiums and ivy trailed down from them. Large stone columns painted green and purple at the bottom, stood like soldiers along the long platform.

"Well," said Scarlet, tapping a long red nail on the arm of the bench, "this is dull. We could do with a bit of entertainment to help pass the time, don't you think?"

She turned her head towards a steep flight of stairs descending from the wide bridge crossing the railway line.

A young man in a smart dark suit was making his way down towards the platform. He had a small black suitcase in one hand and a pale brown leather briefcase in the other.

He was halfway down the steps when his knee suddenly seemed to give way and he stumbled. The briefcase knocked with a clunk against one side of the stairs and then it burst open.

Scarlet crossed her legs, sighed and leaned back into the seat. A sudden freak gust of wind swirled next to the young man.

A snowstorm of papers flew up into the air and fluttered down onto everyone on the platform below. Amy gasped and stood up.

"Sit down, girl," said Scarlet.

"But—"

"I said sit down. Do as you are told."

The young man stumbled again. This time the black suitcase sprang open. Clothes and bottles flew out and spread themselves down the stairs—the bottles clinked and rolled down the steps and across the hard, concrete floor.

Amy could hear the man saying some rude words, but she couldn't really blame him. Why on earth had both of his cases burst open?

People on the station didn't seem to know which way to turn. Paper was flying about everywhere. An elderly man with a walking stick stooped forward to pick up a few sheets that had landed near to him, but his stick slipped. He lost his balance and he was suddenly on his knees on the platform.

Amy stood up again.

"The poor man," she said. "I must—"

"You must do nothing of the sort," said Scarlet. "Sit down."

In the next few minutes, Amy watched all sorts of new incidents. A little boy who was trying to reach some of the billowing paper nearly fell onto the railway lines. He was grabbed just in time by his very cross mother. The elderly gentleman with the stick was surrounded by people and handed a very hot cup of tea by the station porter, which he immediately spilt onto a woman's hand. People were running about trying to retrieve the fluttering paper. Two young girls collided, and a teenage boy crashed backwards and fell into one of the flower troughs.

Amy couldn't be sure, in all the commotion, but she thought she could hear her aunt humming a tune, a little laugh interrupting it for a second here and there. She couldn't be sure...

The young man sat down on the cold station steps and, with a dazed expression, he pulled together some of the spilt contents of his case. He looked up every few seconds at the mass of swirling paper. Amy wondered if it might have been an important project—maybe something really important. Well, whatever it was, most of it was lost now or covered in dirt or blown away from the platform and caught in amongst the bramble bushes and fences at the sides of the railway track.

Scarlet stood up and pushed the trolley with the cases towards the edge of the platform.

There had been no announcement about the possibility of the train arriving but, sure enough, the train slowly chugged around the long sweeping bend of the tracks and squeaked to a halt. The brakes hissed and a strong smell of diesel fumes puffed out into the station.

Scarlet sniffed and crinkled up her nose. Amy, however, liked the smell of trains. It reminded her of holidays with Mum and Dad and trips to Dorset. She wished she was going there now, and she wished she was with Mum and Dad and not with this strange, very cross woman fussing again about her bags—even though the perfectly nice station porter was trying his very best to help her.

Amy sat in a seat next to the window with her back to the engine of the train. Scarlet sat opposite and plonked a bag onto the table in between them. Amy rested her head against the top of the soft seat and pressed her hand against the cold glass of the thick window. She wondered how long it would be before she would see this station again. She wished she dared to squeeze out of her seat, run along the train, push open one of the heavy doors and jump back onto the platform—home to Mum and Dad.

It was no use. She didn't even have a proper home, did she? Only a half fallen down shell of a house covered in horrible muck. She tucked her knees tightly under the seat and traced patterns on the thin strip of rubber at the bottom of the window.

A woman outside in a uniform blew a whistle, waved a green flag and marched off down the platform. The train lurched forward in a juddering way and then it stopped again. Scarlet breathed in hard then she reached up and twirled her hair onto the top of her head into an untidy knot. She stared out of the window, her eyes blazing, and she drummed her fingernails onto the table.

Amy realised that the train had started to move. It was very smooth. Everything on the station started to speed past and then—whoosh, they were out into the open countryside. Amy looked around to see if the young man with the broken cases had managed to catch the train, but she couldn't see him. In fact, she couldn't see anyone else at all. They seemed to have the carriage to themselves.

Scarlet looked across at Amy.

"Well," she said, with a thin smile. "I expect you are feeling quite nervous and excited about all of this, aren't you?"

Amy bit her lip and realised that she felt absolutely terrified. What was she doing on this train? Why had she agreed to come? Her birthday was almost here. Mum and Dad should never have agreed to this. Amy's birthday had always been the most special day of the year. Why had they sent her away just before her very special day? It couldn't possibly be right.

She remembered all the awful things that had happened. They came swarming into her mind and she tried to blink back tears. The flood, the business with Charlotte and Simran, Mr Carr turning strange, the injury to her arm and poor little Neddy-Knock-Knees. It was terrible and somehow, although she couldn't say why, she knew that Scarlet was responsible. And now—here she was on a moving train with this dreadful, frightening woman taking her miles away. Miles away from normality and away from everything that was safe.

"Halewood School is quite exceptional," Scarlet was saying. "I think you will get a surprise."

Amy looked down at the railway tracks racing along and wondered how many miles it was between her home and the far away school. She thought about Simran and Charlotte and wondered what they were doing at this very moment—wondered if they were thinking about her. Probably not, she thought.

Scarlet opened her bag and took out a small blue bottle. She placed it onto the table in front of her.

"Perfume," she said, raising her eyebrows. "My favourite one. Here—give me your arm."

Amy hesitated for a moment and then slowly straightened her left arm and laid it flat across the table. Scarlet roughly pushed up the sleeve of Amy's jumper. The scar from the accident at school on her forearm was still red and angry looking.

"Oh, for goodness sake," Scarlet said, pushing the arm away. "Give me the other arm."

Amy reluctantly pulled up her other sleeve and stretched out her right arm. Scarlet smiled briefly and looked hard at the back of Amy's hand, especially at the straight blue line running across it to the tip of her middle finger. She traced the line with her own finger up and then back down Amy's arm. Then she smiled again. The perfume was cold and the smell, overpowering. It made Amy cough.

"Nice, isn't it?" said Scarlet.

Amy waved her arm about in the air. "It's very strong."

Scarlet glared. "But nice—isn't it?"

The perfume seemed to engulf the two of them in a bubble. Amy reached down for her blue school bag.

She pulled out a small green book with a plastic cover. It had a white daisy decoration on the front.

"What have you got there?" asked Scarlet, her eyebrows pulled into a frown. Amy hugged the book. "Mum bought it for me," she said. "To keep a diary of my trip—of my short time at a different school—so that I wouldn't forget it."

Scarlet started to laugh and then stopped herself.

"Oh, you won't forget it," she said, her eyes widenening, "You'll never ever forget it."

Amy felt a stab of fear in her stomach. She knew she had to rise above these feelings. She had to be strong. She leaned forward and wrote the date neatly at the top of the first page in pencil. She wrote 'On the train with Great Aunt Scarlet'. And then she rubbed out the 'Great Aunt' bit of the sentence. 'On the train with Scarlet. On a long journey. I'm going to be at a new school but only until our house is repaired and I can go home again'.

She looked over at Scarlet. Her eyes were closed—she might even have been asleep, but Amy wasn't sure. It gave Amy her first real chance to look at Scarlet—to look at her properly. Her skin was the whitest she had ever seen and as smooth as ice. It didn't look natural. In fact, come to think of it, nothing about Scarlet looked natural or normal. Why had Mum and Dad made her come away from her lovely home with this freaky woman? They knew she was trouble.

Scarlet's nose was straight and slender, her eyelashes long and black to match her hair and her eyebrows were shaped into high arches which gave her the impression of being permanently surprised. Scarlet's hands lay outstretched on the table. Amy leaned forward on her elbows and stared at them. There was a line of blue running across the back of her right hand and all the way to the end of her middle finger. The line was a very dark colour and pulsing strongly. Amy gasped.

Scarlet's dark eyes shot open and then narrowed. Amy gasped again but wished that she hadn't.

Scarlet slapped her hand down onto Amy's book and twisted it across the table towards her.

"On a long journey...to a new school..." she read and then she laughed.

Amy stared out of the window. The train began to slow down and after a few minutes it was standing in another station.

Amy looked out at the bustling platform. She could feel her eyes stinging and becoming watery again.

"You're scared of things, aren't you, Amy?" Scarlet said in a hoarse whisper.

Amy blinked. "I can be brave when I want to. I was brave in the flood."

"But what about the dark," said Scarlet. "What about if there was a witch under your bed or a ghost in the wardrobe?"

"Stop it," said Amy. "Why are you being so horrible? There's no such thing as witches and ghosts."

"Oh. Is that what you really think?"

"Of course." Amy's voice was quavering.

"What if I told you that I was a witch?"

Amy's stomach clenched into a knot.

"Of course you're not a witch," she said with even more of a worried quaver in her voice. "You're a normal person... aren't you?"

"Normal? Is that what you think?"

Amy swallowed and put her hand to her mouth.

"Well, yes," she said weakly.

"Think about it—have things been normal since I arrived at your home. Well—have they?"

Amy thought again about what was left of her house and about the flood.

"The flood made everything different," she said. "You can't tell me that you made the flood happen. No-one can do that. The rain, the weather...no-one can..." Amy's frightened voice trailed off. What if Scarlet really was a witch...

*

People got off the train and then people got on the train. Lots and lots of people got on. The strange thing was that no-one came into their carriage. No-one at all. But then, Amy thought, everything was strange. The world was suddenly a strange and frightening place.

Scarlet leaned forward.

"If I hadn't...if it hadn't been for the flood and the damage to your house and school," she said, "there would have been no reason for you to have left your home."

She leaned back and pressed her lips together and then her mouth widened into a horrible grin.

"And it's very important that you come and live with me."

"I don't know what you mean," said Amy. "You're frightening me. I wish I'd stayed at home."

"Not much point in staying at home with your house washed away—not to mention those two horrible so-called friends," said Scarlet. "They were very mean to you, weren't they? Very mean."

"I've been friends with them forever," said Amy, her voice breaking into a soft sob. "They've never been mean to me before. Never."

"Well," said Scarlet. "Things can change. Even the nicest people and the nicest things can turn nasty, you know. Look at Neddy, and what happened to him."

Amy's heart started to pound, and her hands began to shake.

"Sorry, Amy," said Scarlet with a sniff. "But it's what I do—I make bad things happen."

"But—"

"For instance," Scarlet interrupted. "That man with his dodgy cases at the station. Do you think his misfortune was just by chance?" She paused. "Well, do you?"

Amy thought of the man's papers swirling around in the station—most of them now lost. She remembered his face, so sad. She remembered him sitting on the cold station steps trying to gather up his things. She remembered Scarlet humming a tune. Amy thought about the taxi driver getting on the wrong side of Scarlet. She thought about the exploding tyre.

Amy couldn't speak. Her head felt as though it was spinning. Felt as though her whole life was spinning out of control.

Maybe this whole thing was a nightmare. Maybe in a minute she would wake up in her own little bedroom listening to her mum clattering plates in the kitchen. Barney might be nuzzling at her hand. Maybe everything could be normal again.

Scarlet tapped one long painted fingernail on the table

in a loud steady beat.

"The fact of the matter is that I am not a witch—you will be pleased to hear, Amy. But I am definitely not a normal person as you so strangely put it. I think you probably knew that there was something a bit different about me all along, didn't you?"

Amy buried her face into her arm. The smell of Scarlet's perfume was overpowering.

Amy wished she had her phone. No wonder she wasn't allowed to bring it. Her voice sounded frail and wobbly when she spoke.

"Mum says strange things happen when you are near," she said.

"Well, there you are then."

Amy bit her finger. She didn't want to cry again but she could feel it welling up inside her.

"I still don't believe you. I don't..."

Scarlet thumped the table with such force that everything seemed to vibrate. Amy jumped.

The smell of the perfume became overwhelming and a haze seemed to surround them.

"Watch," said Scarlet, her face angry and her eyes blazing.

Amy stood up.

Scarlet hissed at her. "Sit down."

Scarlet took a long inward breath, leaned back and closed her eyes in concentration. She spread her long thin fingers on the table and pushed them towards Amy. The skin was like white tissue paper—the line to her middle finger was becoming darker and darker.

Scarlet's breathing became noisy, rasping.

The hands began to change—the fingers started to scrape across the table. They curled inward and looked fat. The elegant red nails became thick and black. The whiteness of the skin became wizened, full of deep lines and darkened to a dirty yellow and then green. The knuckles looked more and more gnarled and swollen.

Amy gasped and tried to move. She couldn't. Tears sprung into her eyes and her ears were buzzing.

After five minutes, every single thing about Scarlet was different. Her black hair was stiff and spiky, her thin nose now looked like a lump of misshapen bread dough. One eye had swollen up and turned purple as if she had been punched, her face was green and covered in strange lumps, her lips, thick and dribbly and her teeth, yellow—stained with black streaks.

Amy tried to speak. She couldn't.

Scarlet—was this still Scarlet? Her body was shrunken. Old. Scarlet's beautiful clothes were hanging from the withered body in draping folds. The blubbering lips curved back into a hideous smile and when a laugh came from her, it was the worst cackle—a proper witch's cackle but— she wasn't a witch. Was she?

Well, whatever she was—witch, monster, sorceress. It didn't matter. The creature that was sitting before Amy was hideous and terrifying.

The monstrous Scarlet stared across at Amy, the swollen eye glittered with moisture. She smiled a horrible crooked smile and then, with another cackle, her lumpy head fell forward onto the table and she was motionless.

CHAPTER 15

Invisible Horses

*A*my didn't know what had happened. She seemed to be waking up. But she couldn't remember drifting off to sleep. She shivered as she woke.

Scarlet was stretching out her long white fingers, filing her red nails and humming a little tune. Her ivory skin was as stunning as ever—perhaps even more stunning than before. It was gloomy outside and heavy rain was lashing against the window. Little rivers of water were dancing across the glass.

Amy felt groggy, as if she had been ill. The train was

clattering along, and the carriage was noisy. What was that noise? What was that smell?

People. It was people. When did they all get on? They were wet people in smelly wet clothes. The carriage was full of chattering people. People rustling newspapers and magazines, people chomping on sandwiches and pasties, people fiddling with computers and unzipping bags.

Amy scrunched her eyes up, opened them as wide as she could and blinked across at Scarlet.

"I think I had a bad dream," she said, shaking her head with a puzzled expression. "A very bad dream. You were in it. You changed—"

"Don't be fooled," interrupted Scarlet, taking a lipstick from her bag. She tipped her head back, widened her black eyes and then leaned forward. Her voice was cold.

"It wasn't a dream."

*

The rest of the journey went past in a blur. Scarlet said they would be getting off the train in under an hour. Amy couldn't understand where all the time had gone. Had she been asleep for hours? Maybe she had.

Scarlet didn't speak again about what had happened. Instead, she talked to Amy like any normal person might.

"Look at the colour of those trees," she said, pointing. "So many different shades of green. Would you like a sandwich? We've got egg and cress, or tuna."

She even had a chat to a lady and her young daughter sitting on seats near to them.

"Oh, yes, we've travelled a long way. From the south... yes, it is a long journey, but it's been quite comfortable, hasn't it, Amy. Oh, you two are going to North Yorkshire too. Lovely part of the world isn't it? My favourite county—especially the wildness of the moors."

It was almost more frightening for Amy to hear Scarlet talking like this. It was as if the rest of the awful, ghastly events had never taken place and that everything was as nice as pie—totally normal.

Scarlet called ahead on her phone to let Clarke, her 'butler', as she called him, know the time of their arrival.

Amy wondered if Scarlet would let her use the phone to call home but after only a second of thinking about it, she knew for certain that the answer would be no.

*

Clarke was waiting at the large bustling station of York. He was a kind looking older man with a cheerful smile. He wore old fashioned dark overalls, a checked shirt and a flat cap. His eyes were blue and gentle and as Amy greeted him, it was difficult for her to guess how old he was. She was just happy to see kindness in his face and eyes.

The rain had stopped, and the sun lit everything up.

Clarke sprang into action as soon as he saw Scarlet. He removed his cap and bowed slightly.

"Good afternoon, Miss Amy," he said. "Welcome."

Amy held out her arm and shook his hand firmly. And it was then that she felt a strong bolt of unmistakable electricity tingling through her body, down her arm, into her hand and to the kind man standing before her.

Clarke looked momentarily stunned. He closed his eyes and looked quite shocked. He blew out his cheeks and went pale. His eyes blinked in a strange way, almost as though he had just woken from a deep sleep.

Amy looked puzzled. She frowned and shook her head. She quickly glanced over at Scarlet who was fussing with the bags and not paying them any attention. After briefly closing his eyes again, Clarke bit his lip and then seemed to recover. He smiled warmly at Amy and rolled a trolley into place ready for the bags and they were soon walking out of the station, through the crowds and towards a long line of taxis. The pavements were shining—still wet after the rain but now quickly drying in the late afternoon sun as it burst through the clouds.

Clarke heaved the trolley past the first few taxis and a little further along the road. That was when Amy saw the horses.

A boy of about fourteen was standing tall and strong between two beautiful huge black horses, their bodies shimmering in the sunlight, their manes and tails as soft as feathers. He was holding onto thick brown leather reins. He wore dark green cord trousers held with strong braces. His light brown shirt was rough and open at the neck. His boots looked well-worn, scuffed and laced tightly up to the ankles.

"Good evening, Madam Scarlet," the boy said. "Hello, Amy. I'm Peter."

Scarlet just nodded towards him and walked past the horses to a stunning dark red and gold carriage. She flung open the door and climbed in.

Amy looked around at the ordinary taxis. No-one at all was looking at this incredibly strange sight. Some of the taxi drivers were leaning on their cars and chatting to other drivers. People were getting into the taxis. Couldn't they see the horses, the carriage? Why weren't people staring in wonderment?

Amy looked at Peter. His blue eyes shone, and his face creased into a broad smile. His hair ruffled in a sudden gusty breeze. He reached out his hand and touched Amy lightly on her right arm. A crackle of electricity exploded between them.

"Hello—" he started to say but then he staggered forward slightly, put his head in his hands and groaned. His eyes flickered strangely and his face turned red, then back to normal and then red again. He let out a little surprised sound and quickly clasped his hand to his mouth.

Amy didn't know what to do. She reached out her hand to his shoulder to steady him and he seemed to stagger again, his eyes wild with unexplained surprise. Amy waited anxiously, wondering if she could help him. But, after a few moments, Peter seemed to be restored and well again.

Clarke came from behind the carriage. He and Peter exchanged a look that Amy couldn't understand. Their eyes were wide, and they looked shocked. Then they both nodded, and Clarke put a finger to his lips, closed his eyes and shook his head.

Amy spoke quietly to Peter. Her voice was full of concern.

"Are you all right?" she said.

Peter closed his eyes for a long moment, his face still and serious. Then his face broke into a smile once more.

"It's okay, Amy," he said. "I'm fine now."

Amy felt that something important was happening. Those few minutes standing alongside Peter and Clarke were special somehow, but she didn't know why.

She glanced around.

"Can't anyone see us?" she asked.

Peter looked over towards Scarlet. He pressed his lips together and shook his head slightly.

Amy tried again, whispering. "Can't anyone see us?"

There was a moment's pause.

"Hasn't Madam Scarlet told you?" Peter said quietly. "I'd best not be saying anything just yet then until she tells you herself."

"Tells me what—" Amy tried to whisper but a sudden piercing screech interrupted her.

The stiff window of the carriage was being forced down.

Scarlet poked her head out.

"Come on, girl," she said. "Peter and Clarke have got work to do sorting out the bags. They don't want to be held up by you blathering on. Get into the carriage and be sharp about it."

Peter's body stiffened at the sound of Scarlet's voice. His face reddened again. Clarke marched along to the door of the carriage, opened it carefully and pulled down a step for Amy.

"This window needs oil," Scarlet said, her face in a scowl. "Didn't you hear that awful noise when I opened it?"

Clarke nodded.

"Sorry, yes, I'll attend to it the moment we get to your house."

Amy stood on the step. The carriage swayed slightly. She hesitated.

"Oh, for goodness sake," Scarlet said, her eyes blazing. "I don't need you holding us all up."

Clarke supported Amy's elbow and kindly helped her up into the carriage. Amy felt a small electrical charge pass between herself and Clarke and he let out a quiet gasp.

Amy sat down opposite Scarlet on a soft leather seat. Everything inside the carriage was dark red or gold. It was beautiful and the smell of leather was strong and lovely. The seats were red with gold stitching and smooth velvet arms and headrests. Soft red curtains were pulled back at the windows by thick gold cord and deep red carpet covered the floor and ceiling. Amy couldn't hide her amazement.

"Wow," she said, and noticed a faint smile play around Scarlet's lips.

Amy leaned back. The carriage smelled of leather and something else as well... she wasn't sure. A hint of Scarlet's perfume, polish and newness. But it seemed to be old. It should have smelled musty, but it didn't.

Amy became aware of Clarke and Peter climbing aboard outside and within a second or two, the carriage was on its way.

She could hear the strong sound of the horses, clip-clopping along the hard road surface, past thick ancient walls, shops and houses. Soon they were out of the city and Amy noticed that the sound of the horses' hooves had changed. She saw that they had left all the buildings and hard roads behind. The horses were now moving swiftly along a smooth country track. She could hear the muffled voice of Clarke speaking to Peter. It sounded as though they were speaking to each other urgently. She couldn't be sure, but if they were, Scarlet showed no interest.

Outside, the countryside was flying past. Sometimes, thick hedges bursting with flowers, sometimes tall trees with thin white trunks, row after row, sometimes old trees with thick pitted bark in dark clumps and sometimes open moorland with patches of scorched black earth and purple heather.

The horses were speedy. Amy expected the carriage

to start rocking and pitching. It might have hit stones or crevasses in the track, but the ride was smooth and steady.

Scarlet was silent.

"Is this your carriage?" Amy asked after a long awkward period of silence.

"Yes," answered Scarlet. She leaned forward, sighed and looked out of the window.

"It's very...it's lovely," Amy said.

"Of course," said Scarlet. "My standards are high. Did you expect less?"

"No...no of course not. It's just..."

"Just what?"

"Well, I thought we'd be getting into a normal taxi or something...not a beautiful carriage like this...and the other thing is that no-one seemed to see us...you know... at the station...as if we were invisible... the horses and the carriage and—"

"You're rambling," snapped Scarlet. "Asking far too many questions for my liking."

She pulled her flowing hair back into a topknot. The white streak wound into it and looked strange.

"You have heard of the word 'trance', I presume."

"Yes," Amy said. "I have."

"There you are then. As you know, I expect, most people go through life in a trance, caught up in their own silly little worlds. They hardly look to left or right. All we have to do is extend the trance and then some things— some of the things that we do—become invisible."

"But—"

"Trancquiescence. There's a lovely new word for you—my own word, actually. Remember it. It quietens people. Makes them unaware of anything off the usual radar. Useful."

"But why—"

"That's enough, girl. I need to concentrate. No more talking. I need to think."

"Can I phone Mum when I get to your house?"

"The landline phones in my village are not reliable so don't count on it. I'm sure your mother and father will be quite sure you'll be all right—knowing you're with me."

And with that, Scarlet closed her eyes and went off into her own weird trance.

CHAPTER 16

The New Girl

*A*my became aware of a different surface under the horses' feet. There was no sound. They were moving along on soft springy grass. Still moving fast.

Dark shrubs and low trees swished and sometimes clattered against the carriage window. Amy started to think about the sort of place Scarlet might live. Maybe a raggle-taggle cottage on its own in the middle of a frightening wood, or maybe a spooky castle halfway up a mountain. Her body started to flood with fear.

The carriage entered a village. It was getting dark, but Amy could see that the village was quite normal and friendly-looking. She hoped more than anything that this was where Scarlet's house would be. Somewhere normal.

She could see many pretty gardens. Rose bushes crept across the walls and honeysuckle was growing up the sides of some of the houses. There was a strong scent of flowers in the air.

The carriage eventually drew up outside Scarlet's house. A full moon hung low in the clear sky. Dots of starlight stretched into the distance away across the tops of the trees. The horses snorted and danced about as they came to a halt and then waited, tied up to a rail, outside a tall thin house.

A single light was blazing outside the wooden door of the entrance. Scarlet slithered out of the carriage and quickly disappeared through a gate at the side of the house without looking back. The gate squeaked and then banged shut.

Amy was left by herself in the moonlit carriage.

There was nothing for it, she thought, but to believe that everything was going to be all right. This was going to be a perfectly normal home, maybe even the new school would be a fantastic opportunity. All the other scary stuff she must push to the back of her mind. She must make the best of what was ahead of her—of course she must.

*

Peter and Clarke were suddenly at Amy's side as she stood in the door of the swaying carriage. Each took one of her hands and helped her to climb down. Again, she felt a strange and strong electrical charge through her fingers as they both gently helped her down the steps.

She thanked them, took a deep breath, and dropped onto the sweeping drive. Her feet crunched onto small pebbles and she looked over at Scarlet's home. It was completely different to all the other houses. Well, of course it was. Neat cottages stretched in both directions but here, in the middle of them, was a strange angular house with a pointed roof and tall chimneys disappearing into the night sky.

Amy could hear the faint sound of animals at the far end of a field opposite and, in the light of the moon, she recognised the outlines of sheep and goats. Chickens were pecking and squabbling with each other in a run on the other side of the fence.

Clarke was now busy unloading Scarlet's bags. Amy was glad to see he was being extremely careful. She didn't want him to get into any trouble.

Peter took Amy's bags down with care and set them on a stone step in front of the wooden door. It had a large frosted window with four separate coloured panes in the centre.

Peter rapped his knuckles against the wood. The window lit up. A girl not much older than Amy looked out.

"Who is it?" she said, her voice muffled behind the

door. Amy couldn't decide if the voice was friendly. She was pleased that it sounded like someone of her own age.

"It's the new girl who'll be staying," shouted Peter. "Open up please. I've got her bags ready to bring in."

Amy shivered. She didn't like the sound of that. She was the new girl. She didn't want to be the new girl. She had always felt sorry for new people coming to Rushworth. She thought it must be terrifying—being made to join a new place when you don't know anyone, and you don't know if you'll fit in or whether a new school might be full of bullies. And here she was in exactly that position. The new girl in a strange place.

*

The door opened and swung back to show a bright hall with square tiles on the floor and a high ceiling. Two girls and a thin woman with a pinched face stood before her.

Amy held out her hand, but the woman didn't move, smile or speak. She just stayed rigid with a sour look and a horrible sneer playing around the edges of her mouth. Amy gulped down an urge to sob.

"Welcome," one of the girls said with a tight, unnatural smile.

"Yes," said the other with a toss of her head. "Welcome. What's your name again?"

Peter sighed. "You know perfectly well," he said and then turned to Amy.

"Amy Harrington—this is Madge, the housekeeper, and her daughters, Angel and Delia. Scarlet has asked them to help you settle in."

"Thank you, Peter," said Angel with a sniff. "The big case needs to go up to the very top floor if you could take it. We will look after Amy from here. You can leave her with us."

Peter looked at Madge and the two girls. He nodded but didn't smile.

"Right you are," he said. He picked up the heavy case with ease and followed Madge up a wide and twisting wooden staircase in front of them, his boots sounding loud.

Angel pushed the door until it was nearly closed, and the three girls stood and looked at each other. The house was quiet and smelled of herbs and incense.

The silence was uncomfortable. Amy stooped forward and picked up the small bag that was left behind and smiled at them.

"Thank you," was all she could think of to say. She hoped with all her heart that they would be kind to her and that they would become friends.

The girls were each dressed in a school uniform of deep red—a smart cotton pinafore dress with a pleated skirt and underneath, a crisp white shirt.

Angel was slender and small. She had very short hair, almost white, and piercing blue eyes. Her skin was perfect—smooth and without a single blemish.

Delia had dark skin, also perfect. Her eyes were brown,

and her hair was shoulder length—red and streaked through with black. She was taller than her sister. She looked strong and muscular.

"So," said Amy with as much confidence in her voice as she could manage. "Is my room on the top floor?"

"Yes," said Angel. "Your room—your very own room— is on the top floor. Don't worry, you won't be sharing it with either of us. That would be awful. We live in the cottage in the grounds."

Amy's spirits lifted. Her own room. A room where she could be on her own. Somewhere where she could have peace and quiet. That would be good.

They could hear Peter's boots on the bare wooden stairs and soon he was standing beside them.

The door opened behind them and Clarke walked in.

"Do you want me to take that other case up, Miss?" he said.

"Oh, no, thank you, Mr Clarke. I can manage this one," Amy said, cradling the small case under her arm. "It's not too heavy."

The girls sniggered and nudged each other.

"It's all right, Miss," said Clarke. "Just call me Clarke. There's no mister needed."

"Oh, sorry, I didn't realise," Amy said. "Well, thank you, Clarke. Thank you very much."

Clarke smiled, touched his hand to his head in an old-fashioned way, then pulled open the door and disappeared into the night.

Angel and Delia crossed the hall to the stairs. Amy started to follow them.

Peter stood awkwardly in the hall.

"Thank you very much for all your help, Peter," said Amy over her shoulder.

But instead of leaving, he hesitated. Amy turned back towards Peter as the two girls disappeared around the bend in the stairs.

Peter and Amy looked at each other intently but didn't speak.

Amy moved the small case from under her arm until she was holding it more comfortably, with both hands. Peter put his hand on her shoulder.

Amy looked into his blue eyes, a questioning and worried look on her face.

"Try not to worry," Peter said, his voice an urgent whisper. "I will help you."

Then, he turned quickly, went out and pulled the door closed with a soft click.

Amy could hear the horses being turned and trotting away, and then there was silence. Her mind was buzzing with questions. What had Peter meant? He had tried to reassure her—but why? She wondered where Madge had disappeared to. She was nowhere to be seen.

CHAPTER 17

The Room

*A*my climbed the twisting wooden stairs. Halfway up was a window. It was beautiful—arched and elegant with stained glass patterns in green and gold around the edge. Even though it was dark, Amy could see in the moonlight that the window looked out onto the side of the house. She could see a large garden and, beyond that, grounds stretching away into the distance.

Tiny lights glittered amongst the trees and shrubs, lighting up dark red rhododendrons and other large blooms. Amy paused and rested her small case on the broad windowsill. She took in the scene and then grasped the handle of the bag and climbed a surprising number of quite steep stairs until she was opposite the door of her room. She found she was quite out of breath and took a moment to steady herself.

She pushed the door, which was slightly open, and it swung open wide to show a much bigger room than Amy had expected. It was at the very top of the house on the fourth floor. Angel and Delia stood quietly at one side.

The ceiling sloped steeply at the edges. The room must be in the roof, Amy thought.

The bed was large and high off the ground with thick woollen blankets and a blue quilted eiderdown. The room smelled nice. A bowl of pink and yellow roses was set on a small table at one side of the bed.

"So," said Angel, stepping forward. "You've been travelling all day, have you—you must be tired?"

"Yes," said Amy, still slightly out of breath. "It's a long way from the south coast but we didn't have to change trains so at least that was helpful."

Delia reached forward, took the small case from Amy and positioned it carefully on the end of the bed.

"Well, we'll leave you to get unpacked," she said. "Your own bathroom is across the landing. Unless you have any questions, we'll see you in the morning."

"Thank you," said Amy. They seemed to be friendly and kind, she thought.

Angel and Delia looked at each other and Angel pulled a face.

"Oh, by the way," said Delia. "Don't worry about that nasty dark cupboard in the corner. Even though some people say it's true, there isn't really a ghost living in it. Good night then."

She linked arms with Angel. They giggled and then walked out of the room, closing the door with a bang.

Amy's desperate attempt at positive thoughts changed in that moment. Here she was in a strange room in a strange house with very strange people. What could be good about that?

The room didn't even have proper windows but sloping glass in the roof and no curtains. Amy could see the dark sky and she didn't want to see it.

There was a large light in the centre of the ceiling under a glass lampshade decorated in green and purple swirls. The walls were rough and pitted—like old cottage walls—and there were three very large knobbly beams of wood across the ceiling.

The floor was wooden boards with a red and green carpet in the centre. Not new, Amy noticed, and a bit threadbare in places.

The bed seemed far too big for one person but at least it looked comfortable and soft—and the room was warm. Beside the bed was a small white table with a bedside light. It had a pale lampshade with fringes. Next to the other table with the flowers was a green wicker chair with a squashy purple cushion on it. Opposite the bed was a heavy wooden chest—a trunk. Peter had put her case on top of it. And next to the trunk stood a large free-standing mirror in a dark metal frame.

Amy sat down gently onto the wicker chair. She pulled off her shoes and stored them carefully against the bedside table and then climbed up onto the bed. She leaned across and put her hand under the delicate fringes of the lampshade and let them flop gently against her skin. The feeling reminded her of her own bedside lamp—her own room with its soft pink bedcover and its little pink wardrobe.

She closed her eyes and rested back against the cushions and pillows. After all day trying to fight back frightened tears, she let them come. First a trickle with her eyes closed and then a deluge with very big sobs. She turned and buried her head into the smooth quilted cover. The cover had a smell—a smell of a strange and different place. She longed to smell the familiar scent of her own soft pillows. She thought of Mum and Dad. They would be worried. She hadn't phoned. She should have asked Peter or even Angel and Delia if there was a phone she could use, but it was too late now. Far too late.

Why on earth had Mum and Dad made her come? Especially now. Tomorrow was her birthday. She should be looking forward to a party and to having a good time with her friends.

It couldn't be right that they had let her come away. She wanted more than anything to be home for her birthday where everything would be safe and normal. Mum knew there was always trouble when Scarlet was around. She thought of the last hug with Mum and the sobs began again.

*

Amy had sometimes wondered about crying. Why did people stop, for instance, when things were so bad or something really terrible had happened?

The sobbing went on and Amy wondered if she might be the very first person in the world who couldn't stop crying. Where would all the tears come from? Was there a never-ending supply?

Eventually, Amy decided that the reason people stop crying is because it is so exhausting. She pushed herself up to the top of the bed, curled into a ball and fell asleep.

*

It must have been the clock chiming that woke her. Amy counted ten chimes. At first, she thought that she was back in her own home and hearing the familiar chimes of the clock on the landing. She could hear the chimes faintly in her sleep but then her eyes opened a little and grew wide. She realised with a sinking heart and a stab of fear, that she was in the strange new room. The chimes were faint and quite nice too. She tried hard to keep calm and to imagine the time, very soon, when she would be back home, listening to her own clock chimes.

The light in the ceiling with the purple and green shade was too bright and hurting her eyes. She leaned across and fumbled awkwardly under the pale lampshade, feeling groggy from being asleep and, with a soft click, she switched on the bedside light. She shuffled across the bed, the quilt ruffling up beneath her, and thumped down onto the floor. She crossed the thin carpet. The floor was hard beneath her feet. She let out a slight quivering sob but then took a deep breath, reached up and switched off the main light.

The room was suddenly full of shadows. She was tempted to put the bright light on again but instead, she quickly crossed the room, bounced onto the big bed, pulled her knees right up to her chest and heaved the heavy covers up to her neck.

Her eyes darted around the room. Door, walls, long mirror, wooden chest, bedside table, flowers, wicker chair, lamp, carpet, cupboard. Cupboard!

There it was—the cupboard in the corner. It was under the sloping roof. One side of the top of the door had been cut into a slope to fit but the worst thing was that the door didn't fit. Not really. It was dark around the edges and it was quite obvious that the door had never properly fitted even though it had a keyhole and an enormous key. It would never have been able to lock properly. Amy could tell.

This was very bad. Amy wondered if the cupboard had a light, whether she could fling it open, put on the light and see that it was the most normal cupboard in the whole world with nothing to worry about. But what about the ghost...what if there really was a...

"I wish you were here, Barney," she said, her voice quavering and her eyes filling with tears. "Then you could be ready to pounce, couldn't you?"

CHAPTER 18

The Horrible Cupboard

Time passed and Amy tried to breathe steadily and keep calm. She closed her eyes and tried to hum some of the songs that Mum had been singing to her at home, but it made her feel sad, so she stopped and just lay quietly.

At first, she thought she imagined a knock at her door. It was so late.

But the knock came again.

Amy nervously slithered down from the bed, walked across to the door and slowly opened it. Angel and Delia were standing in the dimness of the doorway in white nightdresses that came right down to the floor.

"We saw your light was on," said Angel. "We were just wondering if you were all right. Do you know what time it is?"

"Your eyes look red and puffy and you obviously haven't been to bed," said Delia with a wrinkle of her nose. "You've still got your clothes on."

Amy felt embarrassed and ashamed. Could they tell she'd been crying? What must they be thinking? Should she just tell them the truth?

"Well, we might as well come in for a few minutes," said Angel, her eyes widening and shining. She padded across the floor in her bare feet and clicked on the main light, then she gathered up her nightdress, swirled across to the bed and leaned up against it. Amy sat away from her on the green wicker chair. She could see her reflection in the long mirror. Her eyes looked red-rimmed and tired. She was pale and frightened. She forced a weak smile.

"I...I was so tired after...the long journey...I just laid down on the bed and I fell asleep. The sound of the clock chiming woke me up."

"Oh yes," said Delia, swirling into the room. "The village clock. Quite noisy, isn't it—but you'll soon get used to it." She danced and twirled around in front of the long mirror, laughing and throwing her head back.

Amy watched her and then felt that the pause in the conversation was going on too long.

"Is your cottage nice?" she said.

"Of course," they said together. Delia danced in circles over to Angel and they nudged each other.

There was another awkward silence.

"So, what do you think of your room?" asked Angel.

"It's very...quite cosy really. I'll have to find somewhere to hang my clothes, I think. Maybe I can fold them up and keep them in that wooden chest if it's not full already."

Angel jumped up onto the bed and wrapped the quilt around her feet and legs. Delia followed.

"You could hang them up in the cupboard if you want," said Angel, her eyes widening. "It's big. Plenty of space for...clothes and stuff."

"But I haven't even started to unpack—I thought I would do it tomorrow."

"We could help you," said Delia. She jumped down from the bed. "Come on. Let's see how much space there is in this lovely cupboard."

Amy felt afraid. Delia held her nightdress up in one hand and walked slowly across to the cupboard.

"Gosh," said Angel. "It's ages since we've looked in that cupboard. Absolutely ages. All I remember is that it's big and very, very dark."

"Has it...hasn't it got a light?" asked Amy, trying to hide the tremor in her voice and also trying not to let more tears spill.

"Can't remember," said Angel. "The door is wonky though and a bit creaky I think."

Delia pulled at the ancient doorknob of the cupboard. It

stuck out awkwardly because of a screw missing. Above it
sat the huge metal key in the misshapen keyhole, rough at
the edges. Someone had once tried to paint the doorknob
white but now it was chipped with bits of dirty silver
showing through.

The door groaned open. All Amy could see was
blackness. Tears were threatening to come again.

"Goodness," said Delia pushing her hair back over her
shoulder. "There's a strange smell in here. Like old carpets
or something that's been left out in the rain."

Amy coughed in an effort to disguise her fear.

"Is there a light?" she said, her voice trembling.

Delia looked up to her right and Amy saw her run her
hand across the rough wall.

"Ah, here's the switch," said Delia. "I wonder if it still
works."

Angel was even more wrapped in the quilt now. She
rolled over to the side of the bed.

"Only one way to find out," she said.

Delia clicked the switch and the cupboard flooded with
light.

"Yuk," said Angel sliding down from the bed and
joining Delia at the door of the cupboard. "What a lot of
old junk and a horrible stink."

Amy could see piles of bags and boxes, an old sweeping
brush with a long wooden handle, a bookcase which
looked broken at one end, and heaps of books, some
ripped and some new looking. Dark grey carpet was rolled

up roughly at one side with a pile of jigsaw boxes stacked on top of it.

On the side walls were a few brass hooks holding plastic coat hangers. They rattled when Delia touched them.

"Come and look," said Delia. "Might as well see how much space you've got for your things."

Amy noticed an exchange of glances between the two girls.

Angel was peering into the cupboard.

"Oh, look," she said. "There's a little door at the back—not very big. I wonder where it goes to."

Amy pretended to yawn.

"I'll check it all out tomorrow," she said.

"Let's put your case in," said Delia. "And then we can see if the trunk is empty."

"It's okay," said Amy, suddenly feeling unbelievably weary. "If you'll help me tomorrow, that would be great."

But Delia was already heaving at the case.

"Come and help, you two," she said. "It weighs a ton!"

"Come on," said Angel. "Let's help. She'll break her foot if she drops it."

Angel grabbed one end of the case.

"We can't lift it on our own," she said to Amy. "You'll have to help."

Amy stood up quickly, walked across and pushed her hands underneath the awkward case.

"Push it in the cupboard for now," said Delia. "Come on."

The three of them staggered under the weight of the case. Amy thought about how easily Peter had lifted it earlier. They twisted round so that Amy was at the far end of the case and had to stagger backwards.

"Push it in," said Delia.

"Push it in," said Angel.

"Push her in!" they said together.

Amy felt the force of the push and couldn't believe what was happening. Her legs buckled beneath her and she was thrown backwards. The heavy case fell and banged down with agonising pain onto her foot and, as she fell sideways, her face was crushed violently against the rough pile of grey carpet. Its smell was suffocating. One arm bent underneath her and the other was flung outwards. Her hand hit the broken bookcase and more pain seared into her.

She heard laughing. She managed to turn her head towards the door. Angel had the long sweeping brush in her hand. She lurched forward, jabbing the brush towards the light bulb. It smashed instantly. Glass showered down into the sudden darkness.

Amy gasped.

The door creaked shut.

Amy heard the sound of scraping outside and more hysterical laughing. They were dragging the heavy trunk across the door. They were locking her in.

And then—all was quiet.

She was locked in. Locked in the horrible, dark

cupboard.

Amy cradled her hand. She tried to stand but her injured foot gave way and she fell heavily to her knees onto the broken glass on the floor of the cupboard.

She thought she might as well die here in this cupboard. She just might as well die.

CHAPTER 19

Nearly Twelve

It was quiet outside the cupboard for a long time. There was no sound of Angel and Delia waiting for the joke to be over before pulling the trunk away from the door and letting her out.

Amy heard the clock chime eleven and then later another single chime. Half past eleven. Her arm hurt badly, her knees were bleeding, her foot throbbed and she felt desperate.

In the terrifying darkness, Amy realised that in half an hour it would be her birthday. It would be her twelfth birthday and she was the unhappiest she had ever been in her whole life.

CHAPTER 20

The Unbelievable Birthday Surprise

The minutes ticked by. The clock began to chime.
She started humming 'happy birthday' to herself.
She thought of all the other happy birthdays and she
thought she might cry again. She could feel the familiar
sensation of tears starting to come but then, unexpectedly,
she felt different.

A new sensation. One that she had never before
experienced. Her whole body became hot. Her head
started to pound, and her scalp fizzed and burned—

especially in one place. The place where her hair was white—the very place where her hair had always been white.

And then, something else.

As she heard the final chime of midnight, a buzzing began behind her right ear. Loud and as regular as a pulse. Warmth crept down her arm like a river of water. Slowly at first but then speeding up to her elbow along her forearm and across the back of her right hand. All the way down to the tip of her middle finger.

A surge of energy swept across her body and she felt strong.

A sudden piercing beam of light lit up the boxes of jigsaws beside her and then it lit up the broken bookcase and the pile of books. Where was the light coming from? She glanced up at the smashed bulb in the ceiling of the cupboard. She could see it clearly. Shards of broken glass still clung to the fitting. And then she realised. The light— the light was coming from her own eyes.

She no longer felt afraid. The pain in her injured arm and foot had disappeared. Her knees had stopped bleeding and the wounds were totally healed. The painful grazes and cuts she had got on her hand and head when she had fallen against the broken bookcase and rough carpet, had vanished.

Amy stood up, breathed in and held her head high. She briefly closed her eyes and when she opened them, the streaming light had gone. She took two confident steps

in the darkness of the cupboard until she was standing at
the door with the enormous key. She held her hand gently
against the rough wood and, after a few seconds, she heard
the sound of scraping. The heavy trunk was moving on
the other side of the door. The sound stopped and the door
swung open. She was back in the bright bedroom. Alone.

*

The door closed by itself. Amy walked across to the wicker
chair and sat down. She saw her reflection in the long mirror.
    Goodness.
    She stood up and moved closer. The white streak in
her hair was shining as if lit up. It was so bright that it
sparkled. Amy could see the blue line down her neck
throbbing and changing colour. She pulled up the sleeves
of her tee-shirt and saw that the scar on her arm from the
school window incident had completely disappeared. The
other arm was tingling as though charged with electricity
and alive with colour.
    It felt thrilling.

CHAPTER 21

Changed Forever

*A*my was still standing in front of the mirror when the door of the bedroom swung wide open. It was Scarlet. She leaned back against the door frame, her chin in the air. She was wearing silky crimson pyjamas and her jewelled slippers. Her hair was wound up into a top knot kept in place with bright pins.

"So," she said. "It's happened."

"I don't understand, Scarlet," said Amy—her voice sounding strong and unafraid.

"You're twelve, Amy. The age when it happens."

Scarlet looked a little nervous. She didn't come into the room but just stood, slightly awkwardly, in the doorway.

"You had better come in and explain," said Amy.

Scarlet breathed in noisily and then walked across to the chair and sat down.

"Do you feel different?" she said, her eyes shining and her voice excited. "Can you feel it? Your power? Look at your hair, your arm. You're one of us, Amy—a rarity. I need to help you to manage it and get used to your new situation. That's why you're here. That's why you need to be with me."

Amy narrowed her eyes. Scarlet was slippery. She couldn't trust her, but she knew that what she was saying felt right. She felt transformed. Different. Powerful, strong and brave. What could be happening?

Scarlet put her hands together, leaned forward and looked straight into Amy's eyes.

"All you need to know for now, is that you have inherited something very special and at this moment, you are experiencing the start of it. It is marvellous and wonderful, and you are extremely honoured. You will never, ever be the same girl, Amy. You are changed forever."

Amy looked back at Scarlet just as intently but didn't speak. Her body was vibrating with excitement and she felt amazing.

A few silent moments passed and then Scarlet sighed

and eased herself back into the chair as if nothing at all had happened.

"Well," she said, after the long pause. "The girls helped you feel at home, I hope?"

"If you mean Delia and Angel, no, they didn't make me feel at home. They were vile and horrible to me. They locked me in the cupboard."

Scarlet tried to disguise a smirk.

"Well, Amy. I'm sure it was all just a silly joke. Their mother has been my trusty housekeeper for many years. The girls will be coming with you to school. They will show you where everything is and I'm sure you will make some other friends before..." Her voice trailed off.

"Before what?" asked Amy.

Scarlet shook her head.

"Nothing," she said.

"I would like to speak to my mum," said Amy. "I want to tell her that I have arrived safely. I should have stayed with them and I still can't understand why they wanted me to come."

Scarlet stood up. She looked angry.

"You really don't get it, do you, Amy? You've seen me getting into people's thoughts, haven't you? Dear Simran and Charlotte, for instance. Your parents had absolutely no say in the matter once I had..." She hesitated. "Well, once I had persuaded them."

Scarlet smiled, her eyes gleamed and then softened. She pulled the wicker chair nearer to Amy and sat down.

"They are not strong, like you and I."

Amy leaned against the edge of the bed.

"Don't lump me in with you, Scarlet. I don't know what's happening to me, but I do know that I never want to end up like you."

For a moment, Scarlet's eyes widened, her face reddened, and she looked as if she might shout, but her voice was quiet.

She leaned forward.

"Some people in our family have special gifts," she said. "You are one of them. And your aunt—"

"My aunt? I haven't got an aunt. My mum and dad don't have any sisters."

Scarlet shrugged. "Well, you can think that if you want. You might as well go to sleep now anyway—you have a big exciting day tomorrow."

Amy didn't feel tired in the slightest.

"If I have an aunt," she said. "Where is she? What is her name?"

Scarlet looked annoyed. Had she let something slip out that she hadn't meant to?

"If I have an aunt," said Amy, "I insist that you tell me about her." Amy could feel the pulsing in her head again. She stared at Scarlet. Scarlet looked down and then spoke in a whisper.

"Her name was Janice," she said. "Your mother's sister. She's dead."

Amy looked stunned. "What do you mean, she's dead?

What happened to my Aunt Janice? How did she die? Mum has never talked of a sister. She would have told me if she had a sister."

And then, Amy thought of the night of the flood. Mum in the attic looking at the photograph album. The girl with the streak in her hair. That girl with the streak in her hair was her Aunt Janice.

Scarlet looked defiant.

"It was just one of those things. Janice suddenly became ill...she died quickly after that."

"She had a streak in her hair," said Amy. "I saw photographs on the day of the flood. She looked like me. Was she—"

"Just know that she became ill and died young. That's all there is to it."

"But why hasn't my mother talked about her? Have you wiped out the memory of Aunt Janice? Why would you do that? Was her death something to do with you?"

Scarlet stood up and walked to the door.

"Your powers have begun, Amy. It could take a few days, maybe a few weeks or even months for them to come to their full strength. You need to rest tonight. Tomorrow you will be going to school. I will be watching you. I will be watching out for you."

CHAPTER 22

A Delicate Parcel and a Key

Scarlet didn't slam the door as she left but closed it with a soft click.

Amy felt wide awake.

She looked in the mirror.

Her skin. It was perfect. Her skin glowed and her hair shone—the white streak especially was glistening. She looked and felt transformed—just as Scarlet had said.

She felt charged up—full of energy. She thought she would never sleep but she knew she must.

She opened her small case, changed into her

nightclothes, slipped between the sheets and quickly fell into a dreamless sleep.

*

Amy heard the village clock chiming five o'clock. She was immediately awake and alert. She felt strong. Unafraid.

The sky through the window in the roof was just becoming light and dotted with clouds. Amy could see the thin white trail of an aircraft.

Two hours passed. Amy realised she had spent that whole time snuggled into the soft bedcovers with their strange smell and re-living the previous evening. She knew for sure that it had all happened and wasn't some kind of weird dream. She looked at the blue line running down her hand to her middle finger. She touched it with her other hand and felt tingling like a mild electric shock. It felt good.

It especially felt good not to be the terrified girl she had been yesterday. And that had only been a few hours ago.

Her thoughts were racing. She had spent twelve years of her life as a normal girl and now this. If only she had known. She didn't know that the white streak in her hair meant something. She didn't know that the blue line down her arm meant something. She just hadn't known.

*

There was a tap on the bedroom door. Amy sat up in bed.

"Come in," she said, her voice strong, steady and relaxed.

The door opened slowly and Madge, the housekeeper, stood in the doorway.

She was thin as Amy had remembered from last night. She wore a stiff black dress which rustled as she walked into the room.

"I've brought your school uniform," she said without expression. "I've been instructed to wish you many happy returns of the day—today being your birthday."

She laid a dark red pinafore dress and white shirt neatly at the bottom of the bed and placed a pair of sensible black lace-up shoes and thin black tights next to them. A yellow canvas bag with a long strap also lay on the bed.

"I'll be serving breakfast for you in the parlour downstairs shortly," Madge said, still without expression. "Poached eggs on toast, and milk. I will expect you by eight o'clock."

Madge nodded curtly and began to walk towards the door. Then she turned and her lip curled as she spoke.

"Just so you know, don't expect me to be a friend to you," she said coldly. "It's just extra work for me. Anyway, your games kit, pens, books and pencils are in the bag."

She sniffed and turned away again. "My girls will be taking the trouble to show you round at the school," she said over her shoulder. "I hope you will appreciate it."

Amy felt like laughing but controlled the urge.

"Thank you, Madge," she said solemnly. "I will be down to breakfast promptly at eight."

*

Amy's bathroom across the landing was a pleasant room. It was large. In the centre was a deep bath with claw feet. The floor was tiled in blue and white and it felt warm. Above the basin was a wide mirror and under that, a glass shelf.

Amy locked the door and sat for a moment on the edge of the bath. She opened her wash bag and the simple smell of her soap was almost too overwhelming. She buried her nose into the little bag and thought about home. She would speak to Mum today and arrange to go back as soon as she could.

Amy stood up and walked to the basin. The taps were large and old fashioned. Water spurted out in bursts at first and then settled to a stream of very hot water. The mirror steamed up. Amy rubbed at it and was dazzled by the reflection of the white streak in her hair. She was sure it was changing. It was so bright. Everything was changing. Her body felt strong and muscular, she felt taller and energy rippled through her like an electric current.

She washed and dressed quickly and went downstairs.

The parlour was a cool room decorated in dark green with a high ceiling and a second door at one side. The room smelled of herbs and incense just as she remembered from her arrival at the house last night. It also had a musty smell, as though it wasn't used much. A large table was laid with a snowy white cloth. It reminded Amy of a hotel dining room—one of the many she had visited with Mum and Dad.

The table was laid for three. Amy chose the chair next to the window and sat down.

The door opened and there stood Scarlet.

She seemed different somehow—older, maybe shrunken a little, her skin slightly yellow and her hair looked dull.

When she spoke, her voice sounded strange, almost croaky.

"So," she said. "Here we are. I see your uniform is a good fit. It suits you. How are you feeling this morning?" Amy looked across at Scarlet and smiled.

"I feel well and ready for the day, thank you."

Scarlet walked nearer and whispered.

"Your powers will be growing in strength. We can't yet tell how long it will take—but now that you are twelve— you will be one of us."

Scarlet leaned towards a dark sideboard and opened a drawer near the top. She took out a small parcel wrapped in brown paper and tied with blue string. She sat down and put it on the table in front of Amy.

Amy noticed that Scarlet's hand was shaking slightly, and her fingers looked a little bent.

"I want to show you this, Amy, since it is your very special birthday."

Amy looked down at the parcel and then looked at Scarlet.

Scarlet took a deep breath and nodded.

Amy carefully untied the string and the paper fell open. Inside was a delicate black comb with a jewelled top. Beneath it was a thin wooden box. It looked very old and battered. Amy carefully removed the fragile lid.

Inside was a layer of very soft tissue paper and a pink ribbon containing a lock of hair—dark and coarse with a few white strands running through. Amy looked again at Scarlet.

Scarlet smiled.

"This is something unusual, you will agree. It is a lock of my aunt's hair and her comb."

"But they look ancient," said Amy. "They could be from a different century altogether."

"That's because they are." Scarlet closed her eyes for a second. "My aunt was drowned—murdered—in 1654." Her voice faltered. "She was thought of as a witch because of her powers. She was tied to a stool and they plunged her into a deep lake. And they held her under the cold water until she drowned."

There was silence between them for a moment.

Amy shook her head, shocked. "That's terrible," she said. And then she paused.

"But she can't possibly have been your aunt. You must mean that she was a very, very distant relative."

"No. She was my mother's sister. She was my aunt. I

have been very fond of my relatives. You are surrounded by them. Madge, Delia, Angel—even Clarke and Peter. I have looked after those who are related to me down the ages. They have all been useful to me in one way or another."

At Amy's puzzled expression, Scarlet smiled briefly and then stood up. She walked out of the parlour, closing the door behind her.

Amy gently turned the comb over and over in her hand. It seemed to throb with life. Amy knew it was special, but she couldn't understand the logic of what Scarlet had said. It didn't make any sense.

So, thought Amy, still examining the comb, Clarke and Peter are related to Scarlet. Amy knew she would have to think hard about all this new information. It was confusing and mystifying, but it might explain why Clarke and Peter had been able to see the horses and carriage when no one else seemed to be able to. It would make sense if Scarlet had somehow managed to keep track of her relatives. But Scarlet had said they had been 'useful'—a strange way of describing them—and it probably meant that she had used them for her own selfish ends.

At that moment Amy heard footsteps. Clarke and Peter entered the room and, at the other door, a sour-faced Madge appeared, holding plates of food.

Amy greeted Peter.

"Good morning," she said.

Peter smiled warmly.

Clarke took off his cap and pushed it into his jacket

pocket and then sat down.

"Come on, lad," he said to Peter. "These eggs look tasty, don't they? Let's eat up. You've a long day at school."

Amy smiled at Peter.

"Are you at the same school as me, Peter? I wasn't sure if it was just for girls."

Clarke laughed.

"Aye," he said. "You're all in together these days. It was different in my time."

Amy suddenly realised that of course, Peter and Clarke must be related. They had the same blue eyes and the same shaped chin.

Clarke looked over at Madge who was standing by the door, still with a sullen look on her face.

"These eggs are champion," he said, grinning and holding his fork in the air. "Just the job."

There was suddenly a commotion outside.

"Oh, darn it," said Clarke pushing himself up from the table. "Excuse me, Miss," he said.

Madge disappeared and Amy found herself alone with Peter.

"Is Clarke your grandfather?"

"No," he said quietly. "My parents and my grandparents are dead. Clarke is my Great Uncle. My grandfather's brother."

"So," said Amy. "Here I am with my Great Aunt and you with your Great Uncle."

Peter looked down and then over at the door.

"You must be careful," he whispered. "You must..."

Scarlet was suddenly at the door. She looked angry. Peter's eyes widened and his face went pale.

Scarlet's eyes narrowed.

"Finish your breakfast and hurry up, lad, then go out and help Clarke. Never mind tittle-tattling with Amy. She doesn't need to hear anything you've got to say."

She swirled out of the room.

Peter looked flustered at first but then defiant. He stood up, his breakfast hardly touched.

He bit his lip and then reached into his pocket. He pulled out a long thin key attached to a soft blue ribbon and quickly pressed it into Amy's hand.

"There's a door," he said quickly and quietly. "At the back of the house. You must go through the garden. You will find..."

His voice started to quaver and wobble. He sounded as though he could be drunk. His legs buckled from under him and he crashed to the floor.

Scarlet appeared in the doorway.

"Oh, for heaven's sake. Such a sickly boy. I hope he hasn't been giving you any silly little birthday presents?"

Amy knelt down next to Peter. She held his head in her lap and stroked his hand. She glared at Scarlet.

"Don't be ridiculous," she said. "How can you be so mean and cruel? He hasn't given me anything. Probably doesn't even know it's my birthday—why would he?"

"What are you holding in your hand?"

"Nothing."

"Open your hands. Let me make sure."

Amy could feel the softness of the ribbon in her hand and the coldness of the key.

Scarlet glowered and marched across to Amy.

"Let me see."

Amy wished the key and the ribbon would disappear. And as soon as she had that thought, the softness of the ribbon disappeared, and the key seemed to melt away. She opened her hand and there was nothing there.

"Good," said Scarlet. "Although I still have my suspicions. I believe that boy has outlived his usefulness in my service. Time for him to..."

Scarlet was interrupted by Clarke blustering in from outside and out of breath.

"Them chickens were all over the shop," he said. "Heavens above. What's happened here? Peter?"

"He's perfectly all right," said Scarlet. "Don't fuss."

Clarke's eyes were full of concern.

"But he's—"

"I said don't fuss."

Clarke and Amy helped Peter up and onto his chair. Scarlet sniffed.

"Finish your eggs, Peter," she said. "You'll be late for school. You'll have to take Clarke's bicycle. Angel and Delia will be here for you in a minute, Amy. Peter can catch you up when he's ready."

Amy locked eyes with Peter.

Clarke was shaking his head, puzzled and annoyed.

"My bike's too old and rickety to be safe," he said. "It's too dangerous for the lad to be riding it. The brakes—"

"It's absolutely fine," Scarlet said, cutting him off. "I've told you not to fuss, man."

Amy could feel Scarlet's anger intensely. It was like a red-hot heat in the room.

Peter smiled weakly but, after a minute or so, he seemed quite well and recovered.

Amy wanted to ask him a hundred questions—about his warning, about the key, the key that had somehow disappeared from her hand and got into her pocket. But Scarlet was too near, and there was a loud knocking at the door. Angel and Delia had arrived.

CHAPTER 23

The Bike

The girls acted as though the mean and horrible events in the cupboard last night had never happened. They linked arms with Amy as they walked through the village and out into fields, chatting and laughing as if they had known her for years. Their yellow school bags were slung over their shoulders just as Amy's was.

It was over half a mile to the school. After the village, it was all downhill just like it had been to her old school in Boswell, but this time the countryside road was narrow, and the footpath kept disappearing. The three girls now walked in single file next to tall hedges. A few cars swished past.

Amy kept at the back and not too close. She could see Angel's slender body and Delia's thick hair weaving along in front of her. Maybe today wouldn't be so bad. But she knew in her heart that today could be bad. It could be very bad.

The country lane soon joined a steep main road. Cars were streaming down the hill towards the school. The pavement was still narrow. She noticed a big group of boys and girls coming along behind them. They were whispering but her ears could pick up the sounds as though they were speaking in normal voices.

"It's that new girl," one was saying.

"Good," said one of the boys. "This could be a laugh."

"Hope she had a happy time stuck in a cupboard all night," whispered another.

Amy turned to face them.

"Good morning," she said. "Nice to meet you all and—"

But they didn't find out what she was going to say next because Amy's face changed to an expression of horror. Someone was hurtling down the steep hill on a bike towards the main road. It was Peter. Faster and faster on the dangerous old bike. The front wheel was wobbling. He wasn't going to stop.

In a split second, Amy wheeled round to see a black taxi careering down the main road at speed. The taxi was going to hit Peter. Amy felt heat racing through her body. She turned towards the group who were still laughing and whispering—not knowing anything about the terrible scene unravelling behind them.

She turned again and this time concentrated on the taxi. The warmth in her body increased until she felt on fire. The blue line on her arm was pulsing and she became consumed with heat.

The noise of an explosion filled the air as two tyres burst. The smell of rubber was everywhere. The taxi zig-zagged, spun round and came to rest after skidding violently and crashing into a low wall.

Peter's bike shot out into the road a second later at a tremendous speed and out of control. The wheel jammed sideways, hit the kerb and Peter was thrown over the handlebars.

Amy began to run. She ran faster than she could believe possible. She reached Peter's side and bent down to him.

He lay still, his eyes shut. Amy saw his sleeve was darkening with blood.

"I need to bind his arm," Amy shouted. "He's bleeding badly."

Amy knew she needed bandages otherwise it could be too late. Her body pulsed with heat again but even in the midst of this tragic scene, she felt calm and in control. The taxi driver was kneeling down beside her. He was pale and shaking. He held out a small first aid box. She opened it to find exactly what she needed.

The taxi driver asked if he could do anything more even though his car was now useless to help. Amy smiled at him.

"We'll manage now," she said. "I hope you are okay."

"Just shocked by what happened," he said. "The lad had a lucky escape. I would've hit him if it hadn't been for the tyres bursting."

Amy looked down at Peter. He was unconscious. Amy felt a surge of emotion as he lay crumpled and injured in the road. This was Scarlet's doing. Amy knew it.

A group of older boys and girls gathered around as Amy eased off Peter's jacket to reveal a long deep cut. She quickly wrapped the bandages around his limp arm.

The bike was a mass of jagged bent metal. The wheels were buckled and smashed. The accident had been a terrible one and Peter could have been killed. Amy thought back to Scarlet's words— "that boy has outlived his usefulness…" This was a deliberate act by Scarlet. The taxi and the bike had been meant to collide.

Well, Scarlet, Amy thought, your plan has failed. And, at that moment, Amy knew that a battle between them was about to take place and that this was only the beginning.

*

Two women were at her side.

"You have acted quickly and well," one said. "Good work."

Amy could hear Peter's groans as he was gently lifted and carried towards the school by the two women and some of the older pupils. He was regaining consciousness and sounded in terrible pain.

"Who are they?" Amy asked.

"Head of the school, Miss Matthews, and her deputy," someone said.

"They will take him to hospital," a girl said, shaking her head. "I have never seen anyone run as fast as you did. It was amazing."

Amy nodded but her face remained serious.

Behind her, the taxi driver was picking up the bike and clearing debris out of the road.

Amy was feeling strong and calm, but her mind was racing again and full of questions. She walked slowly towards the school gates and tried to think it through. She and Scarlet had special powers. But why?

And now, Scarlet seemed different and nervous. She wondered about the lock of hair and the comb, she wondered about the key on the blue ribbon. She desperately wondered if Peter was going to be all right.

CHAPTER 24

Trancquiescence

A s Amy entered the school grounds, she could see Peter. He was sitting on a long wooden seat with Miss Matthews and he was cradling his arm. His face was pulled into an expression of terrible pain and he was very pale.

As Amy walked quickly towards the seat, Peter tried to stand to greet her, but he fell back.

"Excellent that you are here," Miss Matthews said. "Please stay here with Peter. I will just be a few minutes bringing my car."

Amy sat down.

"You look so pale," she said.

"Thank you for bandaging my arm, Amy," Peter said, his voice trembling. "But it's so painful."

Amy put her hand gently on Peter's shoulder. Again, she suddenly felt on fire. Her body was pulsing and shaking slightly, her hand was tingling and then throbbing.

Peter turned to her—his eyes wide. "The pain," he said. "It's gone."

Amy's body calmed.

Peter was beaming and the colour came back into his cheeks.

"Amy," he said. "I think my arm is better."

He started to unwrap the blood-soaked bandage.

"Let me," said Amy. She gently felt for the end of the cloth and carefully peeled it back from Peter's arm. The bandage was in a terrible mess—but underneath, Peter's arm was perfect.

"You have done this," said Peter, turning towards her and grasping both of her hands. "You have got powers. Powers the same as Scarlet's."

"It strangely seems so," said Amy. "I don't know why it is happening, Peter, but Scarlet has brought me here and now I suddenly seem to have extraordinary strength and bravery. More than that," she said, shaking her head and smiling, "I appear to have healed your arm."

Peter glanced to one side.

"Miss Matthews is coming in her car," he said.

Amy could see the car approaching.

Peter grasped Amy's arm.

"Amy," he said. "You are in terrible danger. The key that I gave you earlier. I stole it last night. It opens the door at the end of the back corridor. You must find the summer house in Scarlet's garden because there you will find out the truth. Please, Amy."

Amy nodded and gave her promise. Then she stood up, held her arm in the air and closed her eyes.

She opened them to see that everything was still—frozen. The people walking into school were stopped in motion and the car was not moving. So, she thought, this is Scarlet's weird trancquiescence—the power over people that had been described to her on their journey in the coach. Well, she thought, it is very useful, there's no denying it.

Amy lowered her arm and the world started moving again. The car drew up alongside them.

Miss Matthews looked confused and sat for a moment before opening the door of the car.

She looked at them with a puzzled expression.

"What are you two doing over here?" she asked. "Peter, you should be making your way into school by now."

Peter and Amy stood up. "Good morning," Peter said. "May I introduce Amy Harrington. She is starting here today at Halewood."

Miss Matthews beamed and held out her hand.

"Hello, Amy. Very nice to meet you. I would normally have greeted you at the gate but there was an emergency and I had to..." her voice trailed off. The memory of the emergency seemed to have somehow slipped her mind.

"Anyway," she said still looking puzzled. "It's very nice to see you and I hope you will be happy here at Halewood."

Peter turned. "We're just heading off for registration," he said.

"Excellent," said Miss Matthews. "I hope you both have a very good day." She turned back to her car and scratched her head, still looking bewildered.

As soon as she had driven away, Peter spoke.

"Poor Miss Matthews," he said. "She can't understand why she brought her car over to us. How on earth did you do that?"

Amy smiled but looked surprised herself at what had just happened.

"I don't know, Peter," she said. "I thought it would be easier if there was no memory of the accident—now that your arm is so suddenly healed. It would have been so difficult to explain, wouldn't it? And I seemed to find a way to do it."

"Your powers are incredible, Amy. The only other person with such strengths is Scarlet." He paused. "It looks like you will be a match for Scarlet," he said. "But she is very strong. I just don't want anything bad to happen to you. Please use the key as I have asked. You will be shocked, but I want you to be prepared. I will help you if I possibly can."

Amy nodded.

Peter stopped as they reached a path.

"You need to go that way, Amy. Through the main doors. I go straight on here. Please be very, very careful. I will meet you for lunch."

Amy turned to look at the school properly for the first time. It was nothing at all like Rushworth. It looked old and impressive with turrets and fancy carving in stone along one side. Another part had thin, tiny windows of the type that might be on a castle.

The grounds were stunning—long stretches of neatly cut grass and flowers in huge beds.

She was alone. Angel and Delia were nowhere to be seen. Amy gazed up at the huge entrance with a red and black tiled floor and a giant wooden door. She hoped everything would go well on her first day. She had no way of knowing then, that her first day at Halewood would also be her last.

CHAPTER 25

Poetry and Pain

A tall man with a neat beard greeted her.
"Hello, Amy," he said. "The headteacher has been
called away urgently. I am standing in as her replacement
to welcome you to Halewood. We hope your time here
is happy. I will be teaching you science. My name is Mr
Edgecombe."

"Thank you," said Amy. "Science is my favourite
subject. My last science teacher, Mr Carr was an
inspiration until…"

Amy was thankful that Mr Edgecombe didn't hear her

voice trailing off. He was already weaving his way along the corridor against a sea of pupils coming in the opposite direction.

Amy caught him up.

"I believe Delia and Angel were to show me round," she said.

"They will be in your form," said Mr Edgecombe. "If you stay with them, they will show you the ropes."

He led Amy to a classroom.

"Well, here we are, Amy. Delia and Angel should be waiting for you. This is your form room for registration, and I'll see you second lesson today for science."

He smiled at her and then walked away in the direction they had just come.

"Thank you," Amy called after him.

Amy walked into the classroom. It had been noisy as she approached, buzzing with laughter and conversation. Now, there was silence. Some who were perched on desks, with their backs to the door, spun around.

All eyes were upon her and no one was smiling. Amy wondered, in the intensity of the moment, how she would have felt if this had happened at Rushworth. It would have been terrifying.

Instead of trembling, however, and being on the verge of tears, she felt strong and quite in control.

"Hello," she said. "My name is Amy Harrington. I'm new to the school. Pleased to meet you all."

A member of staff bustled up behind her.

"Right," the woman said. "Sorry to be a few minutes late. Sit down everyone. Ah, you must be Amy. Welcome. I'm Miss Allenberry. I'll sit you near to Delia and Angel. They have told me they know you."

She guided Amy to a spare seat just in front of Delia and Angel. Still no one smiled.

Miss Allenberry walked to the front of the room, noted down everyone who was present and then addressed the class.

"The reason I am late," she said brightly, "is because your English teacher, Mr Lawrence, has had to attend an important meeting so you will spend the next hour here with me."

Amy liked Miss Allenberry already. She seemed pleasant in manner and spoke to the class in a good way.

"Because you are missing English," Miss Allenberry went on, "I have a poetry writing exercise for you."

Amy's heart leapt. She had always loved poetry— especially writing it in English lessons.

Well, here she was in school with a perfectly nice teacher about to do a favourite thing. Just for a few minutes, things could almost be normal.

But then she felt an extra strong pulse of heat down her arm. The stripe running across to her middle finger was hot—reminding her that her body was in the process of entering a strange new phase. She welcomed it and hated it equally. She knew that the streak in her hair would be ridiculously obvious. She just hoped that no one would take too much notice.

Miss Allenberry walked across to the window and picked up a vase. In it was a beautiful red rose. She stood it on a pile of books on her desk.

"Now," she said, with a smile. "I want you all to look carefully at this stunning flower. I will give each of you a piece of paper. Write your name at the top and the heading 'Rose' and then I would like you to write a poem about it. Use your English exercise books to make a rough draft and then write up your finished poem by the end of the hour. I am just leaving the room for a few minutes so please work quietly and with concentration."

Amy couldn't wait to get started. After all the turmoil of the last few weeks, days and hours, here was a chance to spend some quiet time losing herself in an activity that she loved.

She reached into her yellow canvas bag. She pulled out a pale blue book with 'English' neatly written upon it and opened it at the first crisp blank white page. Her pencil case had an assortment of pencils in it.

She picked out a sharp graphite pencil and looked over at the flower. The single stem was long and had several mean-looking thorns. Amy thought she would start by describing the stem.

She wrote one word 'First.' And then she felt the pain.

The top of her left arm was suddenly in agony. She wheeled round to see Delia laughing, a sharpened pencil in her hand.

"Whoops," she said, nudging Angel.

Amy stood up, towering over the two seated girls.

As the pain in her arm intensified, Amy felt anger boiling up. She knew she should sit down and try to calm herself, but rage took over. The memory of the events of last night and being locked in the cupboard consumed her.

Everyone in the class turned to look.

Amy felt a scream surging up. It overwhelmed her and she let it escape her body from the very bottom of her lungs. The piercing high pitched sound filled every corner of the room. Light from her eyes flickered back and forth from Angel to Delia. She raised her right hand into the air. Every paper in the room began to move—slowly at first but then with increasing speed. Swirling and whirling, the papers, books, pens and pencils joined together in a frantic cyclone.

Heavy text books bounced against the walls and windows. The delicate vase and the beautiful rose were swept to the floor. The glass was smashed into a thousand shards.

Every person in the room was screaming. Some were running out of the door.

Amy lifted her hand again and the storm immediately stopped. She closed her eyes and slowly circled her arm across the chaos. Her eyes opened and after only a few seconds, everything was as it had been before. The papers were on the desks, the books back in piles on the table. The vase was solid, standing exactly where it had been, and the rose as stunning as ever.

*

People standing up were looking confused. People outside started wandering back into the classroom looking bewildered.

Memories had been erased. Amy's arm was no longer hurting. She sat down to begin her poem starting with the word, 'First'.

She became entirely engrossed in her poem and the rest of the class were quiet, writing. It was only after Amy had finished her neat copy that she noticed a figure outside the window dressed in a black cape with a hood, and beckoning her. Amy looked at the other people in the class. Some seemed to be looking directly at the black clothed figure but didn't seem to see it.

The person briefly pulled down the hood. It was Scarlet.

The bell sounded for the end of the lesson. Amy put her poem on the front desk with everyone else's and walked out into the corridor. As she passed one of the doors leading outside, she slipped through it.

Scarlet was next to her in a second.

"What on earth are you doing here, Scarlet?" said Amy, her voice angry and almost whispering. "I don't think you should be here."

Scarlet didn't speak for a moment and then her words came tumbling out.

"I heard Peter was in a terrible accident," she said, her eyes wide.

Amy took a step towards her.

"Peter nearly had a terrible accident," she said. "A near miss. That ridiculously dangerous bike with failing brakes went out of control. He was almost hit by a car. Thankfully, he is all right."

Scarlet's lips tightened.

"What a shame," she said.

"What do you mean what a shame?" said Amy, her voice rising.

"I mean what a shame he was nearly hit," said Scarlet in a hiss. "Well I hope you haven't been chatting to him. He has some wild fantasies that boy. You shouldn't listen to him."

"Don't be ridiculous, Scarlet. He's a perfectly nice boy. A lovely kind person. He only cares about my best interests and safety."

"So—you have been talking to him," Scarlet said, her eyes blazing.

"As a matter of fact, I've been busy writing a poem and I'm now on my way to a science lesson."

"There's no need," said Scarlet, flouncing her black cape.

"No need for what?"

"No need for a science lesson. Actually, no need for you to continue at this school."

Amy took another step towards Scarlet until their faces

were almost touching.

"Scarlet, you have dragged me all the way here, miles and miles away from my home and my friends, my dog and my family. Goodness knows how they agreed to send me here. I'm going along with this for their sakes. I seem to have been transformed into having unbelievable powers—which I still do not understand..."

Scarlet held up her hand.

"No," said Amy, raising her voice further. "I will speak. Everything is totally absurd. My powers—your powers— they are unnatural. I was a perfectly ordinary girl and now what am I? A freak—who can alter time, who can change things in a moment, someone who has unimaginable gifts but are they good gifts? Are they eventually going to change me into someone like you, Scarlet? Because if they are, that would be absolutely horrible."

"You should be grateful," Scarlet snarled. "Out of all of the girls who have inherited the powers—yours have been granted to you in the shortest possible time. They are almost at their full strength already so there's no going back. I was going to help you until your powers reached their maximum. It could have taken weeks, even months but you are special, Amy. They have taken no time at all, you are a natural, you don't need me anymore." She paused and smiled awkwardly. "You are one of us."

"Quite frankly," said Amy. "This conversation should not be happening now. When I come back to your house this evening, we can have a proper talk. There are many things I want answers to. My poor parents must be worried to death about me. I have no idea what they must be thinking. They would be shocked to know all that has gone on."

She turned away from Scarlet. "I am going to my science lesson now."

Scarlet grabbed Amy's arm, but Amy shook her off.

"Be under no illusion, Scarlet. I was once frightened of you. Very frightened. But that has ended and I have no fear of you now. You may be powerful, but I can equal your powers. I intend to return to my parents and to leave this place. My only regret will be leaving Peter. Well, maybe he can come with me."

Scarlet's eyes blazed yellow then red. A piercing white light streamed towards Amy, crackling as it came. Amy was thrown backwards but instantly recovered. Her own eyes burned, and light blasted out of them to meet Scarlet's. The light exploded as the two powers pitched against each other. Amy closed her eyes and when she opened them, Scarlet had gone.

Amy cleared her throat, calmly dusted down her uniform, walked back into the school and made her way to the science lab.

CHAPTER 26

Fire

*A*my expected an inquisition because she was so late to the lesson, but her class were only just walking into the lab. Mr Edgecombe was at the front of the room setting up an experiment on a bench, a smile on his face.

Amy made sure that she was well away from Angel and Delia although they showed no interest in her.

"Is the lesson starting late?" Amy asked a small girl with her hair pulled back into a thick ponytail.

"No," said the girl. "Why do you ask?"

Amy shook her head. "I was delayed for quite a few

minutes," she said. "I thought the lesson would have
started by now."

The girl frowned. "But you arrived at the beginning of
the lesson with the rest of us," she said.

And it was only then that Amy realised that her
confrontation with Scarlet must have happened outside of
real time. No time had passed, no one had seen them. It
made sense in the senseless sort of situation she was in.

Mr Edgecombe was gathering together some powders
and explaining how together they could be explosive.

"It's exciting," he was saying. "You will all need to stand
well back as I put a flame to it."

He took out a match ready for his extraordinary
moment but then, even before it had been struck, there was
a huge bang, a blast of fiery heat and dark smoke began
to rise in thick plumes from the science bench. There was
a gasp, and everyone quickly drew back in alarm. A huge
window blind at the side of the room was on fire. Flames
arched up the wall and several paper displays caught
alight.

Mr Edgecombe took a brief shocked moment to realise
what was happening. Everyone took a moment to realise.
But, as soon as they did, the screaming began.

"Everybody—follow the fire drill," Mr Edgecombe
shouted above the screams, his voice shaking. He strode
out into the corridor and smashed the glass of the fire
alarm.

The noise was horrible. The piercing sound of the alarm

filled the room so that nothing could be heard above it. Mr Edgecombe pulled at the heavy fire extinguisher and directed a flow of white foam towards the flames, but it was no use. The whole classroom was now full of fire.

The class was bursting out of the doors and streaming onto the field outside. Mr Edgecombe followed, his face pale and sweaty.

Amy looked towards the turrets on the other side of the school. Smoke was drifting up there as well and students were stumbling out of every door.

Amy closed her eyes. Could her powers have any chance of saving them? Could she stop the fire? As soon as she tried, the image of Scarlet came strongly into her head. Scarlet was laughing. Amy opened her eyes and there she was in the distance, her black cloak swirling around, her eyes streaming light towards the school.

*

It was now a terrible scene. People were crying and staggering about, some with blackened faces and torn clothes.

Amy looked into the crowds of people for any glimpse of Peter. She couldn't see him.

"Tell Mr Edgecombe I'm out of the building, please," she said to the ponytail girl. "I must find my friend—to know he's safe."

Amy ran fast towards where she had last seen Peter. Her eyes darted from left to right, but she couldn't see him. She stopped, leaned her arm against a wall and concentrated. She could see him clearly in her head. He was trapped with others behind burning wood. Two huge beams of wood were alight and preventing them from escaping.

Amy started running again. She was moving across the grass with speed she couldn't believe. Her body was directing her towards a small door at the side of the building.

Smoke was pouring out. She raised both arms and focused everything she had towards the fire. In an instant the sprinkler system began to work, and the screaming alarm was finally silent. Water poured onto the fire and it started to hiss and fizz as it was extinguished. She ran in through the smoke and steam. She could feel resistance on her body. Scarlet was fighting her, but she felt strong. She moved quickly through the charred corridor and to the room where Peter was trapped.

Everything was soaked as the water poured down. Black debris showered across her. She heard shouts and found Peter and two girls cowering in the corner of a room. The fire was out but they were trapped behind a forest of blackened wood and fallen stone balanced precariously above them.

"Over here," shouted Peter, his voice close to a scream. "We're over here."

"Be ready to run out," Amy shouted. "I'm going to lift the wood. Be ready."

"You'll never do it, it's too heavy," one of the girls cried out. "You must run for help."

"She will do it," Peter said. "I will help her." His voice was now in control. He shielded both the girls with his arms.

"Look away," he said. "We will be saved now."

Amy and Peter pushed two huge beams of wood up into the air.

"Now," she screamed. "Now."

Amy's body was straining and shaking with effort. The girls scrambled out as Peter helped Amy to keep the wood above them.

"Run," he screamed. "Hurry. Bring help."

He could see that Amy's strength was beginning to falter as she tried to escape from the weight of the wood. Peter tried desperately to help her, but his own arms finally buckled. He rolled to safety, but Amy slipped and fell on the wet floor and the beams and stone came crashing down upon her.

The charred splintered wood and broken stone was pressing down and she was struggling to breathe.

Peter strained with every fibre of his body to lift the wood, but his strength gave out. He became aware of a strong force behind him, his legs failed him, and he collapsed onto the floor.

Scarlet's manic voice filled the room. The air shuddered in her presence. Her cape swirled, her eyes blazed and locked onto Amy.

"You can't die. Not like this. You cannot die like this.

Everything will be ruined."

Amy's eyes met Scarlet's. She felt her strength starting to fade.

Scarlet ran forward and, with both arms shaking with effort, she forced the heavy beam into the air. Amy pulled herself out, gasping and catching her breath. The huge charred stones clattered away, and she was free.

Scarlet shifted her attention to Peter.

"You," she snarled. "You know far too much for your own good. You don't deserve to get out of this alive. You wretch."

Scarlet's eyes narrowed, closed and then opened wide. Light streamed out of them towards Peter. He tried to stand, to dodge her attack and to fight her, but finally, he was defeated.

The light remained on Peter until Scarlet lost her balance and half fell. Amy's eyes were streaming light and it was burning fiercely into Scarlet's body. Scarlet stumbled again, regained her balance and whirled round.

Her face was grotesque as she spat out her words. "You are not a match for me yet, girl. Rescue your little friend for now but it won't be long...it won't be long..."

Scarlet swept up her cloak but then staggered to one side and fell yet again. Amy heard Scarlet cursing under her breath. She watched her struggle slowly to her feet and then hobble like an old woman away from the charred ruins of the room. Peter and Amy were alone.

*

Amy felt her strength gradually restored. She leaned forward and placed her hand on Peter's head. His eyes opened but he looked frightened and confused.

"You are going to be all right," said Amy gently.

"She's trying to kill me," Peter whispered. "The fire. It's her doing. She knows I'm helping you. She knows."

His eyes closed again, and it was a long while before they opened, and he was able to sit up slowly and recover.

CHAPTER 27

The Summerhouse

Back at Scarlet's house, Amy and Peter sat in the room where they'd had breakfast.

Peter was quiet and still seemed to be in a state of shock. They had walked home slowly but talking all the way about the tragedy and what terrible things might happen next.

It was over an hour before Angel and Delia returned.

"Has anyone..." began Peter.

Delia spoke first.

"No-one has died," she said, her voice shaking. "No-one."

Angel leaned up against the table, her white hair blackened on one side.

"You're a disaster, Amy," she said. "This is the second school to be ruined when you were in it. Our beautiful, gorgeous school. Half of it is burnt to the ground."

"How could Amy possibly be responsible," snapped Peter, standing up. "Don't be so absolutely ridiculous, Angel. They were both horrible accidents. It's terrible for Amy to be caught up in them. You should be kind and show sympathy instead of blaming her."

His eyes blazed with anger.

"Come on, Amy. Let's get away from these two."

Amy stood up and Peter led her down a dim passage and to a thick wooden door. He pressed his hand against it. "You need to open this door and find out what is out there, Amy. It's very, very important."

Amy took the long thin key from her pocket.

"How did you get this key, Peter?"

Peter looked straight at her.

"Scarlet may be powerful and clever," he said. "But I have strengths of my own. I stole it for you."

There was a noise from the front of the house.

"Scarlet," gasped Peter, his eyes widening.

But then they heard Clarke speaking in a loud and agitated voice. He was asking questions, his words tripping over themselves.

"I will go and tell Clarke that we are safe, Amy. I'm

worried though. If Scarlet finds that you have opened the door..."

"Don't fear, Peter," she said. "Scarlet is not here. I would be able to feel her presence."

Peter nodded and then turned in the direction of Clarke's voice.

Amy carefully slid the key into the narrow lock. It turned easily. The heavy wooden door creaked open to the most beautiful garden Amy had ever seen. A large expanse of grass was neatly clipped and perfect. On each side, there were stunning flowers of every colour and a wide stone path running in front. Behind the flower beds, a tall wall of tiny red bricks ran around the whole garden with an arched wooden door set into it. Towards the back of the grass was a neat fence with a small gate. Amy quickly walked towards it. To her surprise, beyond the gate was a wild and messy tangle of flowers and shrubs but it was still beautiful. The smell of yellow roses was almost overwhelming, and the shrubs rustled as if to greet her. There were so many yellow roses. Many more than she could count.

She opened the gate and gently pushed the roses to one side. She found herself standing at the door of a white summerhouse, the door firmly shut. Amy expected it to be locked but when she turned the small metal handle, it opened.

Inside, there was a colourful armchair and a large old wooden box with a thick leather strap across the top and hanging down the front. Nothing else.

Amy touched the box briefly but jumped back as a powerful pulse of energy surged across her hand, through her arm and into her body.

She took a breath and sat down on the chair. She knew this was important. Peter was right.

Amy pulled the heavy chair next to the box and sat very still, looking intensely at it. Then, she grasped the leather strap and opened the lid. She let it rest gently against the white wood of the summerhouse and stared inside.

The box contained another, smaller box of exquisite wood. Amy gently removed the top of the small box. It was full of pieces of folded paper each with a few written words. At the very top of the papers was the delicate tissue paper and the pink ribbon containing the comb and lock of hair belonging to Scarlet's aunt. Amy tried to imagine the comb in the hair of a real person, and she found she could easily see a picture of the woman who had owned this beautiful jewelled decoration. Her heart was breaking at the thought of the terrible death she had endured.

Amy was swept away in sadness for several minutes, but she knew she couldn't remain here in the summerhouse for long.

She looked again at the beautiful box of folded papers and tried to guess how many there were. Definitely ten. Maybe more. One of the papers at the top was new and crisp. The writing on it read: *'Amy drowned, aged twelve. The very last girl.'*

Amy's heart was pounding. She took the paper into her hand, unwrapped it and a lock of hair tumbled out, wrapped in red ribbon. She knew at once it was her own auburn hair. She saw the streak of white running through it.

Another paper in the box said, *'Janice drowned, aged twelve'* and then a date a long time before Amy was born. She unwrapped the paper and looked at a lock of hair folded inside. It was dark but with white strands amongst it and tied in blue ribbon.

Janice, Amy's aunt. This was a lock of hair from Aunt Janice—her mother's sister—and she had died. Drowned when she was twelve.

*

The other papers were yellow and delicate looking. Each had a name and a date. All in the same handwriting. All young girls. All young girls who had died age twelve. More than ten girls who had died and Amy had no real way of knowing how many—she didn't dare touch the ones underneath. They looked as though they might fall apart.

Amy stared ahead of her, in shock and sadness at what she had discovered and realising the terrifying conclusion—it was Scarlet's intention that she should die. That she should drown. All that was missing was the date.

She thought back to breakfast, to Scarlet's slightly withered hands, to her skin—older and drier looking. She thought about her stumbling and falling after the effort of lifting the wood in the fire, how she had screamed that Amy could not die 'like this' and how she had hobbled out of the room—her body bent and shrunken. Amy came to the startling realisation that Scarlet was dying and losing her powers. It all seemed so obvious now. Scarlet must take the powers for herself but, for her to do that, the new person with the powers must die. Aunt Janice had the powers, so Janice had to die. And all the other young girls going back centuries had died. They had died because Scarlet had murdered them—drowned them. And when they died, Scarlet had taken the powers again for herself. Amy came to a horrific understanding. Scarlet was hundreds of years old. Hundreds.

*

She gently wrapped the locks of hair, placed them back exactly as they had been, slowly closed the lid of the small box and then she gently lowered the lid of the bigger box. Her thoughts were tumbling in confusion. The writing on the paper had said, 'the very last girl'.

Could it mean that she was the very last girl to have the powers? Why would that be? If Amy was the very last girl and Amy died, would that mean that Scarlet would live on forever? There were so many difficult and terrifying unanswered questions.

Amy stood up, moved the colourful chair back to where it had been, closed her eyes and felt the incredibly strong electrical surge of power filling her body. She felt afraid but she also felt angry and defiant. Scarlet could not take her life away. She would fight her. She would fight her, and she would win.

*

Amy walked out onto the soft grass and looked around at the beauty of the garden. She thought of her family, of Barney and of her once lovely home and the gorgeous village of Boswell. She thought of the warmth of the friendship she had been so fortunate to have had with Simran and Charlotte, how she had excelled in her studies and how the world was such a wonderful place. No wonder Scarlet could not bear to leave it. She had protected her powers and her life but in the most terrible and cruel way. She had taken away the futures of all the other young girls.

This could not be Amy's fate. This time Scarlet would not succeed.

Amy heard a scraping noise. It was coming from beyond the arched wooden gate. Amy knew, even before she got to the gate, that horses were what she would find. The wooden gate swung open and there they were. A row of neat stables with the heads of the horses looking out at her. They were stunningly beautiful. Their black coats were shining and their eyes bright. She recognised them as the wonderful horses from her journey in the carriage—the horses that no-one else seemed to be able to see.

They seemed to know her as she walked across. She stroked the soft nose of the first horse and talked to him quietly. Then she buried her face into his strong neck, closed her eyes tight and wondered how she could possibly fight all the power she had seen in Scarlet. But she knew that she must do so and with every ounce of her strength and with all the powers that she had inherited. The first thing to do was to get away from Scarlet, to get away from this house. The horse nodded and turned towards her as if feeling her distress and she almost felt his understanding and willingness to help.

Amy heard the gate click and saw Peter and Clarke entering the stable area. Their faces were troubled and serious.

Peter was soon at her side.

"We are ready to help," he said. "You must get away from here because you must now know that you are in terrible danger. We will ride with you to the station and put you on the train. You can go home—get away from Scarlet. Be with your family for now until the time is right to fight. Clarke and I are experts with the horses."

"But will I be able to ride?" said Amy. "I have never ridden a horse."

Clarke smiled kindly. "Be assured that you will be a superb horsewoman. You will be amazing."

Peter put his hand on Amy's shoulder.

"Clarke and I will be outside at first light. You must be ready. You will not need anything but good warm clothes and courage."

The thought of riding was exhilarating and terrifying in equal measure, but she knew that, for now, she had to get away from this brutal woman and save herself. She closed her eyes and summoned up all her new strength to be the bravest she had ever been.

Amy left Peter and Clarke with the horses and quietly re-entered the house. She quickly climbed the stairs towards her room. She stopped at the arched window and looked out. She gasped. At the side of the house was the bent figure of Scarlet in her dark cape. She was leaning against the wall, her whole body straining with effort.

Amy was transfixed. Her own body started pulsing as Scarlet turned and glared up at the window. Amy felt her legs start to buckle and begin to crumble beneath her. At the same time, Scarlet threw off the cape and straightened up. She threw one arm up into the air and screamed. As Amy's strength faded, Scarlet was restored. She soon looked almost the same as the very first time Amy had set eyes upon her.

Amy forced herself up the rest of the steep wooden stairs to her room at the top of the house and closed the door. She walked across and fell heavily onto the high bed. The lids of her eyes wearily sank down until she felt a desperate need to sleep.

For now, Scarlet had stolen her strength.

CHAPTER 28

The Final Girl

When Amy woke some hours later it was dark and very quiet. She looked at the stars through the skylight window. She knew immediately that the terrible weakness and tiredness that she had experienced earlier had disappeared and now she was herself again. She felt the blue line pulsing in her arm and, as she looked around the dark room, light streamed from her eyes. It was good to feel strong and in control but, equally, the aching longing to be back at home and to be ordinary Amy Harrington again was almost overwhelming.

Amy clicked on the bedside light and sat up in the bed.

Her mind flooded with the danger she was in and she tried hard to think of how she could escape.

She was thinking of the horses, of Peter, of her home, of Barney. If she could connect all these positive thoughts, maybe she would survive. Those thoughts, however, were interrupted as she felt the strong and unmistakeable presence of Scarlet.

The bedroom door swung open.

Scarlet didn't wait for an invitation to enter. She marched straight in and sat down on the wooden trunk opposite the bed.

Amy was not shocked or startled. It was almost a relief to face her.

Amy looked for any sign of yellowing skin, a stoop in her body, a shake in her hand—any sign at all that her power was weakening. But there was nothing. She looked amazing.

Scarlet stood up. Then she sat down again as if trying to collect her thoughts and work out what she wanted to say.

"Your powers will be complete in only a few hours," she said, with her chin lifted and her face set in a sneer. "Whether you like it or not, and I am guessing not, you are the last girl to inherit this gift."

Amy slid off the bed and stood to face Scarlet.

"You may well see it as a gift, Scarlet, but to me it is nothing more than a curse. Since you arrived, my whole life has turned upside down. Everything I love has disappeared. You clearly see it as a wonderful thing that I have inherited these strange special abilities and powers, but they are nothing to what it is to be an ordinary girl with a family and good friends and a home."

She took a step towards Scarlet.

"I can see that your own strengths are fading and that you want to take away what I now have. Well fine, take them, Scarlet. I will gladly give them to you."

"No, no, no," Scarlet said, shaking her head and laughing horribly. Then her face became serious, her eyes narrow.

She spoke quietly.

"No, Amy—it cannot work like that. Once you have inherited the powers you cannot just choose to give them away. They belong to you now. You have no idea what you could do in the world. You have the power to control many things and your life will be transformed for now. If you were to live, you will live forever—for you are the last girl."

Amy remembered the words on the paper wrapped around her lock of hair.

"What do you mean?"

Scarlet closed her eyes, sighed deeply and then glared at Amy. "Every family, down the generations has passed on the powers to me beautifully. Always another daughter— just like you, Amy. And with each new special daughter, my powers have increased. Every new girl has helped my powers to grow. Each new girl who I have taken into the water."

She paused and spat out the next words.

"Someone I have to kill."

They stared at each other and ripples of invisible energy passed between them—but Amy pressed her lips together and stayed silent.

"But you, Amy," Scarlet went on. "You are the very last girl and there will be no-one else now. The powers stop with you. After hundreds of years—the powers stop with you."

Scarlet jutted out her chin.

"Are you not shocked? Afraid?"

Amy walked across to the wicker chair, sat down slowly and spoke quietly.

"I know the terrible things you have done, Scarlet. The terrible selfish things. You have stolen the lives of so many innocent children and wiped the memory of them so that their family could not even grieve their loss. And not to bring goodness into the world—no—only to create chaos and evil. You are a horrible and vile person, Scarlet, and this time—even though your life depends on it—you will not succeed."

Scarlet looked stunned and her defiant look faltered.

"My aunt," she said, with a slight tremble in her voice. "You might as well know, since it doesn't matter. My aunt was tied to a ducking stool all those hundreds of years ago. If she had survived the drowning, she would have been branded a witch and would have been condemned to die anyway and, if she was innocent, she would drown."

Scarlet stood up, slowly walked across to the wall and

leaned up against it.

"I dived into the water. I was twelve years old. I took the hand of my aunt as she drowned, and she gave me what I now have—incredible powers and strengths. Power and strength to get my revenge on the world for what they did to her. Little did I know that the powers would fade. But it became obvious what I had to do, and as time has gone on, I have become stronger. My powers have grown and grown. They have increased with every generation. It has been thrilling for me to avenge the death of my aunt and I have never failed her. Never."

Scarlet pushed herself away from the wall, took a step forward and tilted her head up. Then she fixed her eyes on Amy.

"And now—you are the final girl to come into the water. Why do you think you are here? Why do you think I have brought you close to me? Once your powers come to me, I will live forever. I will be immortal. And it will be complete."

Amy stood up and spoke calmly.

"The last girl?" she said. "How can you be so sure?"

Scarlet smirked and momentarily closed her eyes. Then she set her steely gaze on Amy once more.

"You forget that I have been alive for long enough to know how this finally ends," she said quietly. "I have known since you were born, the moment I saw you. There was always going to be a final girl and I have waited. I have waited all these long years and now, here you are. There will be no girls after you, Amy. Either you live on forever, or the gift is passed to me." She paused, lowered her gaze and then she almost whispered. "I think we both know who it will be."

Amy shook her head.

"Don't be so sure, Scarlet," she said. "I may be the one who keeps the powers—the one who uses them to do positive things in the world. I will fight you and you know I will."

Scarlet shrieked with laughter.

"Ha! You would probably just let the precious powers go to waste by doing some stupid good deed—pouring away these wonderful strengths that you have been gifted. But I will not let that happen. I am watching you every second. Your powers are immense. More than any other girl has had. But they can easily be lost. They must be protected, kept safe as I have preserved them over all these years."

Scarlet pressed her hands together and grinned.

"The powers are for me to take," she said, her voice rising. "And not for you to fritter away on some fanciful idea. Without any doubt, any doubt at all, the ending to this story is the one I have always been sure of. And it is the beginning of forever for me."

Scarlet took another step towards Amy then raised her arms until the room filled with the sound of loud crackling electricity. Blue sparks arched up to the ceiling, bounced off the wooden beams and fizzed against the walls.

She shouted above the noise.

"I have never failed. I will not fail now. Your strength is a match for me, but you will not, you will never, ever defeat me."

Scarlet flung open the chest and took out huge coils of strong yellow rope. She twirled it around, laughing and screaming. The cords twisted around Amy, pinning her arms to her sides even though she fought it with all her strength. It snaked around her legs and she fell to the floor—struggling to resist and feeling desperate.

Scarlet picked up Amy and threw her roughly onto the bed.

"Tomorrow," she said, with her face almost touching Amy's and her eyes blazing.

"Tomorrow, we go to the water."

Scarlet looked triumphant. The electricity blasted and crashed around the room once more and Scarlet swirled out of the door. Amy heard the sound of the door locking as if by a hundred locks and she was left alone, scarcely able to move. She stopped struggling and lay back, trying to relax as best she could and to work out how she could free herself from the suffocating ropes.

CHAPTER 29

Come Home, Amy

The feeling of not being able to move was terrible. Amy knew that fighting against the cords around her was the last thing she should do. It would only make things worse.

She closed her eyes and summoned up the new strength she knew lay deep within her. She began to think of her home, of her mother and father and Barney. She felt calm and her whole body softened against the smooth covers on the bed. The rope around her legs and arms began to loosen slightly and she could breathe more easily.

She looked up to the skylight and the dark night beyond. The stars twinkled and Amy imagined her mother looking up at the same stars. The very same stars. Thoughts of her mother filled her mind and then she gasped as she heard her mother's voice. The yellow cords around her body loosened again. Her mother was speaking to her. It was not in her imagination. Her mother was speaking to her and she sounded upset.

"You must come home, Amy. You are in terrible danger. I have remembered. I have remembered so clearly. My sister, Janice, who was never in my mind until today. It was Scarlet. I know now that Janice was drowned, and she was drowned by Scarlet. I believe you can hear me, Amy. For a time today all my memories came back—the terrible things that happened. Scarlet is a wicked person. She bewitched your father and me. She must have—we would never have let you go."

Amy heard her mother crying and then she heard the unmistakable sound of Barney. He was barking and whining.

Her mother was speaking again.

"We don't know where you are, Amy. You must try to come home. To escape."

The ropes loosened again and with supreme concentration and effort, Amy pushed the yellow loops away from herself and onto the floor where they fell into a pathetic heap.

Amy spoke. "Mum," she said. "I am in terrible danger.

Scarlet is ready to take me into water and the same fate is waiting for me. Scarlet has made you forget—but her powers are starting to fade, and she is losing her grip on you and your memory. She was unable to stop you remembering Janice today. Your beautiful sister."

Amy stared up at the stars. "Mum, I am the last girl, but I have new strength—unbelievable strengths and powers. I am a match for Scarlet and even though she thinks she will win, she will not."

Amy screwed up her eyes. "Mum, I am missing you and Dad and Barney. All I want is to come home and for us to be together again and for this nightmare to end. I will escape and be with you. You must believe me, Mum. Scarlet does not know how strong I can be, and I have help. My dear friend, Peter, will help me and his Great Uncle, Clarke. They will help me to safety even though it will be hard. Don't give up on me, Mum because I am ready to fight."

Amy tried to keep her mum in focus but gradually she faded and as the sky started to turn into a misty light, the stars disappeared, and she could hear her no longer.

Amy jumped down from the bed and tried the door. It was locked.

CHAPTER 30

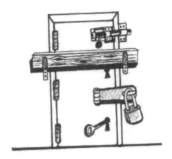

Prison

*A*my focused all her attention and power on the lock. She forced her concentration towards the door. She could feel the resistance immediately and she was knocked backwards so hard that she fell onto the floor. Scarlet's prison was too strong.

Amy imagined Peter and Clarke preparing the horses. She could see them in her mind's eye. But here she was—trapped.

She turned her attention to what she would wear for

the journey. She had to believe she would and could defeat Scarlet. She had to get away.

Soon Amy was dressed in jeans and a jumper and she put out her warm blue jacket. She tried the door again and this time she was thrown back towards the bed by bolts of electricity.

Amy knew she must think. She must think how to work her way out of the room and towards freedom waiting for her outside.

CHAPTER 31

A Way Out

The situation seemed impossible. Scarlet had made any escape out of the door to the stairs out of the question. Amy knew that Scarlet would have almost exhausted herself by creating such a strong prison.

Amy climbed up onto the bed and hugged her knees. She closed her eyes in deep concentration. There must be a solution.

The door of the cupboard in the corner was slightly open. Amy remembered how terrified she had been when Angel and Delia had pushed her in and smashed the light so that she was left in total darkness.

She jumped down from the bed, walked quickly across to the cupboard and opened the door. She stared up at the thin sharp fragments of glass still clinging to the light fitting in the ceiling. The cupboard was as horrible as she had remembered. Dark and full of rubbish. She stood in front of it and her eyes started to water a little and then light began to stream from them. It was an amazing feeling. The light swept across to the old carpet, the pile of books and jigsaws, the broken bookcase…and the small door at the back. A door at the back. Another door out of the room. Amy let out a little gasp. She focused her eyes and all the light on the tiny door. She turned back, collected her jacket and forced her way forward through the muddle of things in the cupboard. She was nearly at the back when she heard screaming.

She recognised at once the desperate voice of Scarlet on the other side of the main door of the room. She was unable to enter. Amy realised that she was almost certainly being stopped by the strength of her own previous success at creating a fortress.

Amy didn't wait a second longer. She pushed herself towards the small door. With hardly any effort at all it swung open and Amy squeezed through. It was tight, but the door led to a long, narrow flight of steps and Amy quickly made her way down, even though they were steep and slippery.

She could still hear Scarlet screaming, but the sound

was becoming faint and muffled the further down she travelled. The dark stairs opened up unexpectedly into a tunnel. The light from her eyes helped her to find her way. Amy could hear water dripping high above and it smelled damp. Underfoot were rough stones and pebbles. She travelled quickly across them towards a jumble of ivy and thick branches which gave way easily as she pushed against them and she emerged into the soft, misty early morning light at the front of the house. And there, a little way in front of her, were Peter and Clarke with three beautiful black horses.

Amy ran towards them but immediately felt the presence of Scarlet who staggered out from the house looking terrible. She was bent almost double, her hair in a mess of knots and her voice screeching.

"No other girl has ever defied me like this," she screamed. "It is an outrage. I will not tolerate it."

Amy felt the strength in her legs begin to falter and Scarlet began to straighten up until she was at her full height. She quickly wound the wild hair into a pile on top of her head. The powers were moving back to her, but Amy still felt strong.

The horses were circling. Coming nearer and nearer to Amy. Peter looked afraid but determined. Clarke was holding a stirrup out for Amy.

"Come on, Amy," he said, his voice almost a whisper. She pushed her foot into the stirrup, lifted her body and sat astride the horse as Clarke fumbled to adjust the leather straps.

A bolt of blue electricity knocked Clarke from his feet. He stumbled forward and fell, face-down onto the coarse gravel. His face was a mass of cuts and his hands were bleeding.

Scarlet screamed with laughter.

"You traitors," she yelled. "Don't for a minute think that you will be spared."

Clarke heaved himself up onto one knee. His eyes were wide with fear.

Scarlet was thrown backwards as a bolt of electricity from Amy hit her. Peter quickly and expertly wheeled the horses around. Amy was now feeling very strong. The horse beneath her was beautiful, his blackness gleaming and his muscular body made Amy feel that their escape was only moments away.

Clarke was still on his knees. Peter put out a hand to him, but Clarke roughly pushed it away.

"No, lad," he said. "I'll catch you up. Get on now. I'll be beside you in a minute."

Peter hesitated and once again held out his hand.

This time Clarke shouted roughly. "Get out of here, Peter. Get out."

Peter's eyes were wild and frightened. He threw himself onto the horse and then, after a few confused circles, he and Amy galloped away.

Scarlet was still on the ground, but she gathered herself up and, with incredible strength, ripped a long thin branch from a tree. She flailed it at Clarke who tried to defend himself but finally could only cower away. The branch cut into Clarke's face again and again. Then Scarlet threw it down and grabbed at the reins of the third horse. She tried desperately to climb onto him, but the horse reared up, his hooves coming close to the shoulder of the raging woman. She slipped and then regained her balance. She pulled hard on the reins and snatched up the branch. She whipped it across the neck of the beautiful animal. He was bleeding and terrified. Clarke ran between the horse and Scarlet, and he felt the savage sting of the branch across his arms and back. The horse reeled. Scarlet lost her grip and he broke free.

Clarke looked up to see Madge, Delia and Angel running around from the side of the house.

They stared in horror and disbelief at the scene before them. Clarke was bent over, gasping in pain and the horse was in the distance, his wild movements showing his terror and distress.

Scarlet turned and looked at them all. Her hair had become loose from its topknot and blew around her face in a tangled mess. Her eyes were red and wide. Then, she calmed. She stood quietly for a second and then spoke.

Her voice was menacing and low.

"Stand up, Clarke," she said. "Go immediately to the stables and get the carriage. Get it ready now. And you, Madge, can sit up top with him to make sure he keeps to his task. Angel and Delia, you can ride with me. We will all work together to catch that brat of a girl and her treacherous little helper."

CHAPTER 32

Escape

*A*s soon as Amy had got herself properly settled into the saddle, she felt safe. Peter was ahead and they were at full gallop. The ground was flying past—grass, heather, stony paths and rough tracks. Peter was shouting instructions.

"Gather up the reins, grasp with your knees, lean forward. Hold the mane if you need to."

But Amy instinctively knew what to do. The horse was helping her to keep her balance and he felt like a rock beneath her.

A milky sun was sitting just above the horizon and everywhere looked beautiful as the mist lifted.

Peter made sure to glance back frequently and he finally slowed down to a canter then a trot. When there was no sign of Scarlet, eventually they stopped.

"Are you okay?" asked Peter. "You are doing so well. You're a natural."

Amy patted her horse's neck. "He's doing all the work and helping me," she said. "It's amazing to ride like this."

Peter frowned and looked back into the distance.

"You can be sure that Scarlet will not be far behind," he said. "I'm guessing she will take the carriage. But I feel afraid for Clarke."

"Her cruelty is getting worse because she is becoming desperate," said Amy. "But her powers are weakening as mine are stronger. She is dragging them back to herself and I can feel the strong pull—but in every second that passes, I am resisting her force, Peter. I can only thank you more than words can say for helping me."

After a brief pause, Amy looked straight at Peter and told him the truth. "She is planning to kill me by drowning."

Peter bowed his head. "Amy, I know. You are more than special to me. We must fight her—we cannot let her win. This time she must not win."

He closed his eyes for a second and then straightened up and looked ahead.

"We must hurry to the station," he said. "If we can board the train and get away, it will give us a chance to put distance between us. It won't save you, Amy, but the more time that passes, the stronger you will be, and Scarlet's powers will fade."

The horses walked on and then broke again into a canter. They drew next to each other.

"We cannot underestimate Scarlet, Peter," said Amy. "She is still very strong. She will take a less direct route in the carriage, but she has dear Clarke as a hostage. I cannot use my powers to sabotage her while she has Clarke. I fear terribly for him."

CHAPTER 33

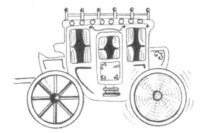

Chasing

S carlet had screamed at Clarke as he tried his best to hurry to get the carriage ready. He plunged his hands into water in the stables and splashed his face, but blood continued to ooze horribly from the wounds he had suffered. He struggled in terrible pain to make the last horse in the stables ready. The injured horse that Scarlet had whipped was still loose, and his eyes were wild with fear—too traumatised to be able to pull the carriage.

Scarlet cursed. She knew that two horses pulled the carriage easily, but now she would have to make do with one—and she knew that it would make her journey slower and more difficult. Madge tried her best to help Clarke, but she was not used to working with the horses and she was nervous around them.

Scarlet sent Angel and Delia to hurry and find food and warm clothes for her. When they returned to the front of the house, Clarke was ready, Madge was next to him and the girls joined Scarlet in the carriage.

Scarlet was looking increasingly furious and desperate. She ordered Clarke to whip the horse and then she settled back into the corner of the carriage, a scarf wrapped around her face and in a silent rage—with Angel and Delia sitting opposite her, bolt upright and in a state of terror.

Clarke did not whip the beautiful horse but encouraged it in his own way by speaking soft commands. The horse made good time, but Clarke knew that Peter and Amy would be at the station long before them.

CHAPTER 34

Waiting

As Peter and Amy arrived into the station, the same strange situation as before unfolded. Trancquiescence meant that no-one at all could see the horses. The station was busy with early morning travellers. Amy felt almost invisible herself and she was glad.

Peter spoke quietly to the horses. He took them to a turn in the road and carefully tied up the reins so that they were free. With a shake of their beautiful heads, they trotted off into the distance and then broke into a gallop.

Peter smiled. "They will find their own way back," he

said. "They are very special, and we have nothing to fear."

Amy watched the horses until they had disappeared. She bit her lip and thought about how strange everything had become. But she trusted Peter and knew the horses would be safe.

The train was not due for twenty minutes. There was nothing to be done. They had to wait in the horrible knowledge that Scarlet would soon be here, and that it could be too late.

An old flat wooden trailer sat in the entrance to the station. Peter and Amy climbed up onto it and let their legs dangle down. It made Amy feel like a little girl again. But here she was, strong and capable with amazing powers.

An old man shuffled past dragging a heavy bag. He looked to be in terrible pain. Amy forced her attention onto him. Her eyes bore into his bent back and she focused her energy onto his broken body. Her hands became hot and the blue line in her arm and hand was pulsing. A brief spark left her and travelled towards the man. He stumbled forward slightly but then he regained his balance and stood up. He was no longer bent. He let out a little sound and then gasped. He looked round at Amy and Peter. Amy smiled innocently at him and Peter grinned and shook his head. The man put his hand to his back and looked both astonished and mystified. His pain was gone. His health was restored. He lifted the heavy bag as if it had no weight and marched forward, his head held high and a wide grin on his face.

"Amy," Peter said. "Look at what you can do. Your gift is going to be amazing. You can heal and you can do great acts of good with the strengths you now possess."

Amy nodded. She thought back to the train journey here with Scarlet and all the terrible problems she had caused on Exeter station. Scarlet had enjoyed using her powers for evil and mischief and to entertain herself by watching the misfortunes of people around her.

"What will happen to me, though, Peter?" Amy said. "Will I live forever aged twelve? The future is a mystery to me."

"You will grow to be a woman," said Peter. "A woman as old as Scarlet—but then you will not grow old like the rest of us. You are the last to inherit the powers and they will be yours to do good in the world forever."

Peter turned to Amy, his eyes misty. "I will die, Amy, but you will not."

Amy was quiet for a few moments.

"I can sense Scarlet is getting near, Peter. The train will be here in a few minutes. I hope we can escape from her for now."

CHAPTER 35

Catching Up

S carlet did not speak for the entire journey to the station. Angel and Delia could see the change in her. Her skin was yellowing and her once bright eyes were dimmed. Her hands looked swollen and wrinkled but the blue line stretching to the tip of her middle finger was still clear and pulsing very strongly.

Clarke saw in the distance the two black horses that Peter had sent home. They were galloping, snorting and throwing their heads back as they came.

Scarlet pulled down the window of the carriage and leaned out. Her scarf and tangled hair flew out in a stream as she watched the horses disappearing into the distance. She closed her eyes and breathed in heavily. A smile came to her lips briefly but, just as suddenly, disappeared.

"Where are we going?" whispered Angel, her voice trembling.

"I think we—" but Delia's whispered answer was cut short as Scarlet's eyes flew open and she glared at the two girls.

CHAPTER 36

Dearest Clarke

*A*my knew that Scarlet was almost upon them. The train had finally arrived and was lazily pulling into the large station. A crowd of people gathered near the edge of the platform. People were getting off agonisingly slowly.

Peter and Amy found seats in a carriage and waited. The platform cleared and the guard walked along blowing a whistle and waving a flag.

With a lurch, the train started to move. Amy took Peter's hand. They were going to get away. The train seemed to inch forward but then, gradually, began to speed up.

They passed through a narrow valley with steep sides. The train was slow again and it was only when they were through the valley, back in the open and travelling past a low hedge that Peter and Amy saw Scarlet's carriage. It was moving fast through a field and parallel to the train lines on a thin gravel track. Clarke looked distressed and Madge, terrified.

Peter stood up. "Clarke," he cried out, his voice almost a sob. "What has she done to him? His face is bleeding."

The carriage was weaving wildly along the track. The horse was covered in white foaming sweat. Clarke was doing his best to calm him by shouting instructions, but the horse galloped on—his eyes terrified. He seemed to be being driven by an unseen force. The unseen force of Scarlet.

Amy could feel the strong pull of Scarlet. She was trying to gain some of the power, but Amy fought back. She forced all her attention on the exhausted horse, willing him to slow down and finally his legs responded, and his pace slowed.

The horse stopped for a moment and then walked on very slowly and with a limp. Scarlet jumped out of the carriage. She climbed up onto a wooden fence at the side of the track, her eyes wide and wild, her body stiff with rage.

And then, with a strong jolt, the train came to a halt. Amy rushed to one of the doors and pulled down the window. She willed the train to start but she could now feel her strength quickly ebbing away. Scarlet's forceful glare was sapping her strength. Amy sank to her knees.

The train started to move forward but excruciatingly slowly. Scarlet stepped down from the fence and edged her way along the track—walking with her head held high. The carriage followed. After a few more metres there was a level crossing where the narrow track crossed the railway lines. A heavy gate swung down across the path of the train and it was forced to stop.

Peter jumped from the train and ran desperately towards his uncle. He saw Madge, Delia and Angel drop down from the carriage. They looked dazed, confused and very frightened. Peter leapt over the wooden fence, onto the gravel, skidding and slipping. He ran, half stumbling, towards Scarlet, but Madge and her daughters had recovered from their confusion and they blocked his way. They quickly gathered around—stopping him from getting near to the raging woman. They were strong and determined as they held him—even though he pleaded desperately with them. He could only watch in helpless terror at what was unfolding before them.

Scarlet was looking about wildly. She bent down to duck under the gate, but Clarke was quickly behind her. He caught her by the arm and twisted her round. Rage and pain were all there to see on his grim face. Dried blood covered his cheek and one eye was half closed.

Scarlet slapped him hard many times. She punched at his face and dug her sharp nails into the wound on his cheek, screaming with hate. He caught a handful of her hair and clutched at her wrist, forcing her arm roughly behind her. She struggled and managed to coil away from him and then she screamed again and blasted electricity into Clarke. He fell back heavily onto the ground as she jumped forward and roughly grabbed the mane of the terrified horse. She forced shocks and bolts of crackling blue lightning into his dark neck. He reared up in terrible pain, his eyes wide and white with terror. The leather straps twisted, strained and split. One finally tore loose, sending the heavy carriage skewing sideways—rocking, pitching and out of control.

Peter howled in despair. He tried to force his way forward and away from the iron grip of the three women. But he was trapped.

Clarke scrambled across the rough ground and tried to roll sideways to avoid the flailing hooves of the horse and the wild runaway carriage, its wheels spinning in a frenzy and the doors now hanging open. The sharp metal edges of the wheels caught Clarke, pinning his legs and slicing heavily into his arm. He wailed in pain and blood started to pour from his injuries. Scarlet screamed with a terrifying cackling laugh and then she raised her arms. The horse reared up and the twisted metal of the carriage rose high into the air before the full weight of it came crashing down onto Clarke. He was crushed.

After a few desperate moments with Clarke screaming and writhing in agony, his body went limp, his eyes open and unseeing.

He was dead.

Peter wailed and sobbed. He was finally able to release himself from the grip of Madge and the girls. He staggered over to the twisted ruin of the carriage. He fell heavily to the ground and pushed himself underneath the tangled wreckage and caught the lifeless hand of Clarke. The body of his dear uncle lay motionless. Peter reached out, put his hand onto Clarke's still chest and he howled and howled in grief.

*

Amy had been collapsed on the floor of the train next to the door. Her strength was all but gone and she knew she could not help.

As she heard the terrible sound from Peter, she felt her strength quickly returning. She flung open the door, jumped down next to the railway tracks and ran across to him. He had pulled himself clear of the carriage and was curled up on the grass, his tight fists forced into his eyes.

Amy desperately looked for Scarlet. She was nowhere to be seen although Amy knew for certain that she was near. She looked into the stunned and startled faces of Madge, Angel and Delia. It was as though they had just woken up. Angel was holding onto Delia's arm and shaking. Madge was leaning against her two daughters with hardly the strength to stand.

Amy looked back at the train. Why had no-one come to help? But then she quickly realised that everything that was happening here was invisible to the other passengers. Outside of normal time. All they knew was that the train had come to a halt, their journey was interrupted, and it was annoying.

Madge finally recovered enough to try and calm the injured horse and release him from the wreck of the overturned carriage. Peter stood up to help and, between them, they finally unfastened the torn leather straps. Peter whispered to the horse. The animal slowly turned and limped back along the track.

Amy used her quickly returning strength to raise the carriage from Clarke's broken body. They all pushed against the tragic wreckage until finally it was free and fell away to one side. It rolled and tumbled down a grassy slope where it came to rest as a tangled heap of metal—the wheels squeaking and slowly spinning to a stop.

Peter cradled Clarke's head in his hands. He looked up to the sky and sobbed in grief.

Angel and Delia sat next to Peter on the ground and hugged him.

"We held you back…for your own good," said Delia, her voice stuttering and tears streaming down her cheeks. "If we had let you go, your life would have been lost…as well."

"We had to save you," sobbed Angel.

Madge walked across to Amy. When she spoke, her

voice was soft and kind.

"We have been under a terrible spell," she said, her voice breaking. "In a trance. Scarlet has had us in her power, but this shock has broken it. Our dear Clarke. We all loved him, and he was everything to Peter. We have all been trapped by Scarlet and we have done some terrible things. I am so sorry."

Amy nodded and placed her hand on Madge's arm but then turned to Peter as he spoke.

His voice was trembling and his face, white with shock.

"What…what can we do? We can't…we can't just leave him here."

Amy closed her eyes. Blue electricity crackled around her. When she opened her eyes, she knew what she must do.

"Peter," she said, her voice strong. "This will be strange, but you must understand that what we are about to do is what Clarke wants for you."

She looked intently into Peter's sad eyes.

"All the goodness in Clarke is going to come to you now. All his kindness and wisdom and his love for you. His beautiful spirit will enter your soul and your heart so that you will always have him with you, and he will be part of you forever."

Peter stayed quietly kneeling beside Clarke's broken body for a long time, his head bowed, and his eyes closed.

Then he looked up towards Amy and nodded. "I'm ready," he said.

Madge, Angel and Delia held hands—their faces
full of desperate sorrow. Amy looked up to the sky, her
expression steady and focused. Her strength had never
before felt so great. She knelt down and put her hand
gently onto Clarke's head and held Peter's hand. A dense
green mist swirled around them all. Peter clung tightly
onto Amy. When the mist slowly lifted, the body of Clarke
was gone.

CHAPTER 37

Sorrow

*A*my lingered for a moment and then ran to the train. Anger was burning through her. She climbed up into the carriage, trying to sense where Scarlet could be. But it was too difficult. Scarlet was on the train, of that there was no doubt. Amy could feel the powers pulsing between them. Finally, she gave up. She sat down and looked out at the scene before her.

Peter was standing but his eyes were closed and his face, solemn. Delia, Angel and Madge gathered around Peter and hugged him in turn.

"I feel different," he said to them. "I feel a great weight

of sorrow, but I can also feel the strength of my Great Uncle willing me on. He wants me to be strong."

Madge bowed her head. "Clarke was a remarkable and lovely man," she said. "The girls and I will never ever forget him. He was very special to us."

Then the three of them turned away and, very slowly, they walked back along the track.

Peter looked up towards Amy and then back at Madge, Delia and Angel. He stood for a few seconds with his eyes closed then he quickly crossed to the train and climbed up.

The door banged shut and he sat down next to Amy. She put her hand on his arm and watched as big tears silently slid down his cheeks.

"I can't believe it," he said. "I just can't believe it."

Amy directed her eyes towards the gate across the railway track and it began to rise. After a few minutes the train started to roll forward and then gradually picked up speed.

Amy and Peter were silent for a long time until Peter turned to Amy and said, "Thank you. I now know that Clarke will always be with me."

"His strength will be yours," said Amy.

Peter took a breath and then spoke quietly.

"What you must know, Amy, is that Clarke and I are related to Scarlet. Also, Madge and Delia and Angel. Her own family of course are long gone." His sad face turned towards Amy. "The truth is, Scarlet is hundreds of years old."

Amy nodded. "Peter, I know that you are all the descendants of her family. She has watched you all being born down the ages."

"Amy, she is ruthless." Peter clenched his fist. "She has picked out those who are helpful to her and discarded the rest. My mother and father and grandparents died in a horrible accident. She knew Clarke and I could manage horses, so we were spared. We were just useful to her. She weaved her spell over us—made us her servants. She's an evil woman, Amy, with terrible power. You have now inherited that power, but she will try to take it from you— just like she has from all the other young girls."

Amy was silent for a few moments. The anger and hate she felt towards Scarlet was as intense now as it had ever been.

"Tell me about your family, Peter," she said.

Peter looked down.

"My parents were gentle people," he said. "They were kind and generous and they were smart. They could see Scarlet was causing problems—many problems—and they started to question her, to challenge her."

Amy nodded. "And Scarlet would have felt threatened?"

"Not even threatened. Just irritated. They were in her way, so she just decided to—" Peter's voice broke off. Amy clasped his hand.

"The trouble is," Peter went on, "that all these terrible memories have only recently come back to me, Amy. Do you remember the day you arrived? As soon as you

touched my arm, my trance was lifted, and all the horror
came back to me and to Clarke as well. Our memories
have been lost these past years. We have been nothing but
slaves to Scarlet. As the powers started to come to you, we
could see her fading but still so strong. We had to pretend
we were still under her spell."

Amy tightened her grip on Peter's hand.

"But she finally realised."

"Of course," said Peter. "We knew that it wouldn't take
long for her to know we had been released from her and
that is why she tried her best to be rid of me. If it hadn't
been for you, Amy, the crash on the bike could have
been the end of my life and that was exactly what Scarlet
wanted. That is what she wanted for Clarke and there, you
see, she has succeeded."

Amy thought of the kind, caring man she had just seen
so brutally murdered, his body crushed and twisted under
the horrible weight of the carriage.

"I wish I could have saved him, Peter. I'm so sorry."

Peter nodded.

"I know you would have saved him if you could.
Scarlet's powers were just too strong in that moment. The
question is, Amy. Where is Scarlet? Where is she now?"

"There's no point in pretending, Peter," said Amy.
"She is nearby—on this train with us. But she will be in
a poor state. All the energy she has used today will have
left her much weaker now that the powers are coming to
me, but she has a way of bringing them back to herself

and regaining strength. We are in a battle. The powers are swinging back and forth between us, but she knows it is only a matter of time before she fades. She knows she will have to act quickly. She will be near to me from now on Peter, until she tries to take me into water for the final time."

Peter let out a little cry.

"We must fight her, Amy. She cannot win. Not this time."

There was silence for a little while and when Amy turned again to speak to Peter, she realised he had fallen into a deep and exhausted sleep.

She bought food from the trolley as it passed for herself and Peter and then closed her eyes. It was a long journey to Exeter and she knew that she must use the time carefully to plan how she was going to survive whatever Scarlet had in store for her.

CHAPTER 38

The calm before the storm

my turned and looked down the train carriage. It was full of passengers. Some were asleep, some were chatting and a few of them were speaking on their phones.

She stood up, eased out of her seat and walked to the end of the carriage. There was no sign of Scarlet. She moved quickly through the rest of the train and was sure that she would know when Scarlet was near, but there was no sign. She made her way back, past Peter, still asleep, and walked to the other end of the train, making sure to look at every seat.

Still nothing.

It was only when she was nearly at the very end of the train that she knew Scarlet must be nearby. She could sense her, but she was not in any of the seats. The only carriage left was locked and used for storing bulky luggage, bikes and other large items. There was a small window at one end. Amy peered in and saw the small twisted shape of an old woman on the floor. Her face was covered, and she seemed motionless. Could she be dead?

With that thought, the twisted shape moved, and Amy felt a slight weakness. She quickly returned to her seat. Now that she knew where Scarlet was, she must act without delay.

She sent a strong ripple of power across the carriage. Every person was suddenly asleep. The girl a few seats down dropped her phone onto the table. Amy picked it up.

The conversation with her mother was emotional but short. Amy had said all she needed to for now.

As the rest of the carriage woke, Peter also opened his eyes.

He talked to Amy for a long time about Clarke. She came to understand how he had helped Peter to learn to get the horses to trust him and to manage them. He told her how he and Clarke had supported each other to cope with the challenging behaviour of Scarlet. His voice broke every few sentences, but he carried on. Clarke had been Peter's rock and his closest friend.

Amy was aware throughout the conversation of the strong pull on her powers. Scarlet was recovering, there was no question.

Peter's words, however, were powerful enough to distract Amy and she realised how much she was coming to care for him.

As the train neared the station of Exeter, Amy knew she had to be brave and strong.

There were going to be a lot of challenges ahead but just the thought of being with her parents and Barney again made her feel as though she could almost faint.

The train finally arrived and juddered to a halt.

Amy scanned the station. It was noisy and busy.

She and Peter stepped down from the train. In the far distance, a familiar group of people were running towards them. At their feet, a ball of black fur straining on a lead jumping up and down with excitement.

"Barney!" gasped Amy.

After a few moments she had Barney in her arms and was wrapped tightly in her parents' emotional embrace.

Amy took a breath and introduced her mum and dad to Peter who bowed to them in an old-fashioned way and they all politely shook hands.

Amy became aware of two others standing nearby. She glanced up to see Charlotte and Simran looking at her nervously.

They both started to speak at once, but Amy held up her hand and walked across to them.

"I know things became strange between us," she said. "But it wasn't your fault."

They looked puzzled and once again started to speak but Amy cut across them.

"These are very strange times," she said. "It is difficult to understand but I hope I can explain it all to you soon. In the meantime, I'm just so happy you are here."

Peter stepped forward.

"Simran, Charlotte, I would like you to meet Peter."

After a few slightly awkward greetings, they all moved slowly towards the exit.

"I've got a big taxi waiting," said Amy's dad. They walked out to where the taxi driver was waiting.

It was only then that Amy looked back.

And there, leaning against a tall lamppost, was a beautiful slender woman in a red dress and an animal print scarf. Her eyes were slightly narrowed, a smile playing around her lips, and she looked as strong as she had ever been.

Scarlet stared intently at Amy. A strong invisible electrical charge shot between them and they both knew that the final battle was about to begin.

CHAPTER 39

Screaming

When the taxi arrived at Boswell, Amy had already been answering many questions from her parents. She tried hard to protect her mum and dad from the reality that terrible danger was so close.

Peter was quiet but Amy felt an enormous amount of strength from him.

Amy asked the taxi driver to let herself and Peter out in the middle of the village. Her mother was unsure. She didn't want to let her out of sight even for a second, but Amy calmly reassured her, and Helen finally agreed, as long as they promised to be at the Craythorpes' very soon.

The devastation of the flood was everywhere.

Peter and Amy walked slowly towards Amy's ruined house. Peter was visibly shocked. There was not really much of it left.

Amy's mind was overwhelmed by thoughts of that terrible day and all the destruction that had been caused by Scarlet. She stood quietly, lost in the memories but then her face clouded with anger and she raised her arms high.

She focused on the corner of the house where the floodwater had hit most ferociously and was most damaged. Her body shook and she held Peter's arm to steady herself.

The house was soon hidden by a dense swirling purple mist. Amy forced all her energy into the mist for many minutes until she was exhausted and fell to her knees.

The mist very slowly cleared.

Peter gasped.

"Amy," he said. "Look at what you have done."

Amy stood up and took a step towards what had once been the destroyed house. It was restored.

The broken windows were repaired, the stones and bricks were in place and the roof was just as it had been before the storm.

"I can scarcely believe what I have been able to do," said Amy with a shake of her head. "Think of all the good I can do in the future."

She turned towards Peter. He was biting his lip and trembling.

"What is it?"

Peter looked at Amy and took her hands into his own.

"Scarlet has never failed," he said. "All the other girls. She has taken them to the water, and she has stolen the powers for herself. I am so frightened for you."

Amy nodded.

"I am very strong now though, Peter, and Scarlet knows she will have to fight. I am prepared to face whatever it is she has planned and even though she is ready to destroy me, I can win—especially with you here to help me."

They slowly turned towards the gentle river running through the village. On the far side stood a solitary figure, arms outstretched and looking straight towards them. It was Scarlet. Her eyes blazed and shone with light. And then a piercing laugh filled the air—louder than any voice they had heard before. It went on and on. The windows rattled in the houses and trees swayed and bent as though they were in a high wind.

Peter let out a cry, but Amy took a step forward, raised her hands into the air and directed her own blazing eyes towards the screaming woman.

The sound stopped immediately. There was a long low hum which faded away to nothing. Everything was still and Scarlet had disappeared.

CHAPTER 40

What is to Come?

eter and Amy walked quickly but quietly back through the village with the terrible image of Scarlet playing on their minds. Amy talked to Peter about what Scarlet had told her—how her powers had grown and grown as she took each new girl into the water through the generations. Amy's eyes filled with tears of sorrow as she thought of all the poor innocent girls. How frightened they would have been, how terrible their deaths. She made a promise to herself and to Peter. With all her new strength and powers, all her courage and with every last breath in her body, she would prevent Scarlet from succeeding. Death in the water this time must be the death of Scarlet.

*

The Craythorpes were very happy to see Amy and didn't ask any awkward questions. They were much more concerned about showing Peter to his own room and making him feel welcome.

After an evening of being together, they all finally went upstairs to their own rooms. Amy sat on the edge of her bed and wondered about what was to come. She hugged Barney for a very long time until he curled into a soft black ball and fell asleep at the foot of her bed.

She felt a mixture of emotions and wished more than anything that the relief she was feeling about being back in Boswell was not swamped entirely by the terror of Scarlet. Her powers were stronger than they had ever been, but she knew that Scarlet was more than ready to match her. She had looked so strong. Strong and confident.

She could feel Scarlet's presence and knew for certain that she was near.

There was nothing for it but for Amy to sleep and get as much strength as she could find to face whatever lay in store.

Amy switched off the main light. The little side light

next to her bed cast shadows around the room. The delicate fringe of the lampshade tickled the back of her hand as she turned off the lamp. Within moments she had fallen into a deep sleep.

CHAPTER 41

Ready to Fight

It was still dark when Amy woke. She sensed immediately that something was wrong. Barney was gone. She dressed quickly and looked out of her bedroom into the dimness of the corridor which ran the length of the upstairs. Her parents' door stood wide open.

As she made her way towards it, Peter appeared.

"Something has happened," said Amy. "I think something terrible has happened. Barney is missing."

Amy and Peter ran into her parents' room. Her mother was not there. Her father looked asleep.

"It's far too early for Mum to be up," said Amy. "This isn't right."

Peter turned and walked quickly towards the door.

"I'll see if she is downstairs," he said. "Maybe there's a simple explanation. Maybe she has taken Barney out for a walk."

He tried to smile but couldn't manage it. He turned and was gone.

Amy walked across to where her father lay. She touched his arm. He didn't move. She gently shook him. He didn't move.

Amy put her hand on his chest. She was relieved to feel his heart beating strongly.

"Dad," she whispered. And then she shook him again and shouted—but she was still unable to wake him.

Amy's eyes lit up and the light scanned across her father's face. She knew that this was Scarlet's doing. Her father was unable to wake, unable to move.

Peter appeared.

"Amy," he said. "I'm so sorry but there is no sign of your mum or Barney in the house."

Amy looked straight into Peter's eyes.

"There's no use trying to pretend," she said. "Scarlet has started her plan to take the powers for herself."

"I'm feeling afraid," Peter said.

Amy crossed to where he stood and took his hands.

"Remember that you have all the bravery of Clarke inside you, and now I am going to give you even more strength because I need you, Peter. We will fight and together we can win."

The streak in Amy's hair sparkled and the blue line in her arm pulsed strongly. Peter closed his eyes as waves of energy ran between them.

Finally, he stood tall and strong, his head held high and his face full of determination.

"Your father must help us," he said.

"No," said Amy. "Scarlet has already made sure that he is unable to help us. He is in a deep, deep sleep—beyond waking. But he is alive, and he will recover. I think Scarlet has taken Mum and Barney to make sure that I will go to where she wants me to be. And that is on the water, Peter. I know she has taken them onto the sea. We must make haste to the harbour."

Peter nodded and looked down briefly. Then he took a deep breath. "I am ready to fight," he said.

Together, they quietly walked along the corridor, down the stairs and, after gently closing the door, they stepped out into the cool air.

CHAPTER 42

Onto the Sea

A wind got up and the weather started to remind Amy of that strange day when Scarlet had first arrived in Boswell.

The sky was dark, and the darkness increased. A storm was in the distance.

Peter and Amy hurried down the steep hill towards the harbour as the sun crept above the horizon. They saw no-one until they arrived at the harbour wall. Far out to sea, a small rowing boat was bobbing about with the unmistakeable figure of Scarlet standing up, arms held high and her head thrown back. Her long black hair was streaming out behind her.

At the other end of the boat was the crumpled body of Amy's mother struggling against tight ropes twisted around her. Barney was jumping around—whining and crying.

Amy looked about wildly. Peter ran to a set of stone steps in a gap in the wall.

"Look, Amy," he cried out. "Another rowing boat. It looks as though it has been made ready for us."

Amy could scarcely contain her fear and anger, but she knew she must remain calm.

She turned to Peter.

"This is what Scarlet wants. This is her way of forcing me out onto the water—her chance to end my life."

Their eyes met.

"Peter, if you are not ready for this battle, I will understand."

Peter pulled his mouth into a grimace and made a fist with his hand.

"Amy," he said. "I am ready to fight with you, for Clarke, for my parents, for my grandparents and for my whole family. To rid the world of the curse that is Scarlet."

He grasped Amy by the hand and they quickly made their way down the slippery steps with the strong ocean smell of seaweed surrounding them and salty spray splashing into their faces.

The small boat tipped sideways as they quickly stepped

into it and then struggled to sort out the heavy oars. The wind was getting stronger and making small waves crash against the side of the wood, making it difficult to control. Early morning light was spreading across the sky, but dark storm clouds hovered on the horizon.

Soon, Peter was rowing strongly through the choppy sea and towards the terrible scene in the other boat.

Amy could see that her mother had blood on her face and looked barely conscious.

As they got closer, her mother's eyes half opened, and she cried out Amy's name in a desperate sob.

In the distance the storm was intensifying. Lightning crackled across the sky and thunder rolled loudly around the bay.

The sea was being whipped up into a frenzy by a strong wind. Both boats rocked and pitched.

Scarlet was standing astride the seating, using her body to make the boat rock even more wildly. Her face was set in a terrifying expression of hate. Barney howled and cried.

Peter struggled to control the boat, but he pulled alongside. Electrical heat crackled between Scarlet and Amy.

Amy stood up but lost her footing as the swell of the sea tipped the boat sideways and she fell heavily. As she regained her balance, a blast of spray from the cold sea stung her face.

Peter cried out. When Amy had recovered herself, she

saw that Scarlet had thrown Barney into the water and was gathering up Amy's mother into her arms.

Every part of Amy was pulsing with the heat of anger. Barney was managing to keep afloat but Amy could see the terror in his eyes.

The struggling body of her mother hit the water, the ropes still tight around her body.

Amy looked at Peter very briefly, pulled her lips together and nodded.

"This is it," she said and dived into the bitterly cold water.

Peter turned the boat skilfully and manoeuvred it towards Barney. He grabbed his collar and quickly lifted the soaking and shivering little dog.

He scanned the water. Amy's mum, Amy and Scarlet had all disappeared beneath the waves. The empty boat was bobbing about forlornly, being pushed around in circles by the increasingly choppy waves. The storm had arrived overhead, and the rain was intense.

CHAPTER 43

The Battle

*A*my swam quickly down towards the disappearing figure of her mother. The water was freezing, and the taste of salt was strong. Everything sounded muffled and her eyes were stinging from the pressure of the cold seawater as she swam down. The shock of entering the water was overwhelming but her mind was focused, and she felt strong. She grasped her mother's arms and forced her energy towards the tight ropes. They immediately began to loosen and then fell away completely. Mum's arms and legs were free. Amy kicked with all her strength and pulled her towards the surface. They both gasped mouthfuls of air as they emerged into driving rain and the noise of the storm.

Amy pushed her trembling mother gently through the tumbling waves towards Peter. She saw him reach down easily to catch her, reassure her, and lift her into the boat.

Amy felt a powerful pull on her legs. Scarlet was dragging her down and down with a terrible force. Amy tried to fight her way back to the surface, but the grip was too strong. Scarlet's grinning face came level with her own. Her hair was streaming out behind her with the white streak as bright as Amy had ever seen it.

Amy struggled and fought but she felt herself begin to weaken and fade. She could feel herself slipping away—the coldness of the sea was folding in on her and her lungs were bursting. Then, from nowhere, a surge of strength ran through her body. She forced her hand into Scarlet's face, grabbed her hair and twisted it hard and, at the same time, sent a bolt of electricity into her body. She saw fear in Scarlet's face as she was stunned and momentarily lost her grip. Amy managed to kick her away, push to the surface and take several deep breaths. Then she swam towards the empty boat.

Amy reached for the rope loops at the side of the boat and with enormous strength, she quickly pulled herself inside.

Her eyes darted across to the other boat where her mother was moaning and shivering, and Barney was quivering and shaking with cold at the bottom under the seats.

Peter shouted a warning, but it was too late. Scarlet

was behind Amy in the boat, rocking it wildly, screaming obscenities and trying to tip them both into the water.

Peter rowed quickly so that the boats were crashing against each other, the wood grinding and splintering. Amy and Scarlet were locked together. Scarlet dragged her fingernails across Amy's face so that blood started running down one cheek.

Peter waited for an opportunity. He lifted an oar and brought it down powerfully towards Scarlet's body.

But Scarlet was too quick. She caught the oar, let go of Amy and swung it with all her strength at Peter. The oar struck him with huge and devastating force across the side of his head. He gasped and then his eyes rolled back. He collapsed and fell back into the boat. His eyes were only half open, staring and unseeing—and he was still.

Amy let out a sob. She turned to see the horrible grinning face of Scarlet.

"His death is everything he deserved," screamed Scarlet as another bolt of lightning blazed across the sky.

Amy directed every bit of her energy and anger towards Scarlet who lost her footing and tumbled into the bottom of the boat. Amy picked up one of the oars and sent it crashing down across Scarlet's back.

Scarlet was dazed for a moment but then turned. She had transformed into the terrifying witch-like creature that Amy had seen on the train. Gnarled hands grabbed Amy's legs and the two of them tumbled again into the frantic waves and disappeared under the water.

The sea boiled ferociously and lit up into a bright white light as Amy and Scarlet fought for their lives. Amy pushed Scarlet beneath her as she came to the surface for a strong gulp of air, but Scarlet kicked and then twisted Amy round and down, trying to keep her under the water.

They were matched equally in strength, but Scarlet had experience on her side. She had done this many, many times before. Amy's need to breathe was overwhelming and her lungs were burning with pain. The agony of drowning was upon her and she finally felt her strength begin to ebb away. The sounds in the water became muffled and a darkness swirled around her.

Scarlet broke the surface for a long breath, returned to the water and pushed her hideous witch face alongside Amy's. Her victory was almost complete.

Amy's eyes were hardly open, but she could see Scarlet's triumph. She was grinning horribly, showing her dark stained teeth. Her bulging eyes were glittering. She threw her head back in glee as she kept Amy under the water for the final few moments.

CHAPTER 44

Ghosts

*A*my's eyes shot open. Scarlet had released her crushing grip and she had disappeared.

Amy managed to find the strength to kick hard, break to the surface and take a few desperate breaths of air.

When she dived again under the water, even though the cold was stabbing her eyes, she saw not one—but many figures. One of the figures was almost invisible but instantly recognisable.

The ghostly form of Clarke was slowly swirling around Scarlet.

Scarlet forced herself to the surface. She gasped a brief gulp of air—her horrible witch face contorted into a terrified silent scream. Then something—someone—was beside Amy. Another ghostly face—but this time, the beautiful face of a young girl. She had long flowing hair lit up at the side with a sparkling white streak. It was the face of Janice. She swirled gracefully around Amy and then smiled and pointed down to what was happening deep below.

Clarke and many other ghostly forms—all young girls—were wrapping themselves around Scarlet. They were dragging her down, impossibly down, into the depths until after several minutes, the witch that had been Scarlet floated limply to the surface and was buffeted by the waves in the boiling sea.

CHAPTER 45

Closed Eyes

Soon, there was nothing left of the old witch, Scarlet. She had completely disappeared.

Amy let herself float on the surface of the water and breathed in many deep mouthfuls of delicious air. The rain had stopped, and the sky was brightening. Waves still tumbled across her face as she was bumped around in the cold, bubbling sea, but she closed her eyes and every part of her body was charged with strength. The powers that Scarlet had lost were now fiercely flooding into Amy.

She felt the presence below her of Clarke and Janice and all the lost girls. They swirled around her like graceful fish in the water and then the faces of Janice and Clarke came close to her own. Amy raised one defiant hand as she was lifted effortlessly out of the water and into the boat by the beautiful ghosts.

Amy's mother was cradling Peter and crying. Barney sat at the other end of the boat, afraid and shivering violently.

Amy reached across to Barney and placed her hand on his soft head. He stopped shivering and sat up, his red tongue lolling out to one side. She moved across to the terrible sight of Peter and her mother. She stroked her mother's dripping hair.

Peter was cold. His hands were limp, his lips were blue, and a trickle of dark blood had dried on his pale cheek.

Amy looked at her mother. Her face was stricken with sorrow and grief.

"There's nothing to be done, Amy. He is dead."

Amy put her hand to Peter's chest. It was still and no heartbeat greeted her touch.

*

Amy stood up. The white streak in her hair was glistening and shimmering. The blue line down her arm was pulsing. Bright light shone from her eyes and electricity sparked and crackled from the tips of her fingers.

Amy looked towards the distant harbour. It was deserted and everything was still. She lifted her arm and the pools of water that had collected in the bottom of the boat were gone.

Amy sat down and spoke to her mother gently.

"Mum," she said. "I think Scarlet is dead. We have defeated her. Janice and the other girls and Clarke—"

"I don't understand," Helen said, shaking her head. And then they both looked down at Peter's limp body.

"Help me to lay him flat, Mum," Amy said. "Please do not be afraid by what you are seeing and what I am about to do. It will be strange, and it may be frightening but I want you to trust me. I have extraordinary powers and I am going to try to save Peter. I don't know if I can. It will be very difficult but all I can do is to try."

Her mother nodded and then held Peter's head as Amy lifted him gently and placed him into the bottom of the boat. Her mother stood up and quickly moved across to Barney. She buried her face into his black coat and then she looked up, her eyes shining with hope.

With a sweep of her arm, Amy calmed the rough sea and a quietness settled over them.

Peter looked peaceful. Amy felt all the love for him boil up inside her. She felt all the anger and burning hate for Scarlet.

She closed her eyes, took Peter's hands, and summoned every ounce of her power into his still body.

She shook violently with the effort. The two of them disappeared into a thick red swirling mist. The boat rocked and spun around. Lightning flashed many times across the sky in an unnatural way and thunder rolled around the bay with tremendous booms.

Many minutes went by. Electricity crackled around the boat until the mist very slowly lifted.

Amy had fallen limp onto a seat near the edge of the boat, her hair in a wild tangle. The white streak had gone. The blue pulsing line down her arm had disappeared. She could barely move. She still held onto one of Peter's hands.

"Amy," said her mother, gently. "Amy."

Amy struggled to raise her head and open her eyes. The enormous strength she had possessed had completely left her body.

She turned her head to look at Peter. His eyes were closed, his light brown hair plastered with wetness against his brow. His lips were still blue, and the trickle of blood had mixed with the moisture in the air and now ran down in a streak to his pale neck.

As the boat rocked to one side, Amy's hand splashed heavily into the bitter cold water of the sea. A ripple of electricity ran down her arm and a bright light struck the surface, disappearing into the depths—still bright and glowing as it sank into the darkness. It felt final.

She lifted her hand and laid it gently onto Peter's cold forehead. Then she managed to sit up and put her hands to his. His body was still and lifeless. Amy's face crumpled in desperate anguish. Her strength was gone. There was nothing more she could do.

*

Her eyes were closed for a long time. She was exhausted and consumed by terrible grief. When her eyes finally opened, she saw her mother shaking her head, her face full of uncertainty and her hand across her mouth.

Barney was jumping forward excitedly.

Amy dared to look down at Peter.

Warmth and colour were very slowly returning to his pale cheeks.

She put her hand to his chest. A faint beat. But a beat. His heart was beating, and he was alive. He was alive.

Amy squeezed his hand and then gently rubbed it. Joy coursed through her body as she felt his hand move and then reach out to her. Then, Peter opened his eyes, looked at Amy and very weakly, he smiled.

CHAPTER 46

Rising

The put-putting of a small boat with a motor, making its way towards them, was becoming increasingly loud. Amy would have recognised the sound anywhere. It was 'Old Salty'.

Only one person was aboard and, as it approached, Amy could see with great relief that it was her father. He cut the engine and pulled the old boat alongside.

"Dad. Dad," Amy spoke as loudly as her weakened state would allow. "You are recovered. You are all right."

The stricken face of her father stared back at her. His eyes were heavy and red rimmed.

"I'm so sorry, Amy," he said. "How could I have slept through all of this?"

Amy shook her head.

"You didn't, Dad," she said, her voice breaking. "It was Scarlet's doing. She kept you unconscious so that you were unable to help us."

David started to secure the boat, his hands fumbling with the ropes. As he spoke, his words were tumbling over themselves.

"I woke suddenly," he said. "It was so strange but, in my mind's eye, I could see you and Mum and Peter and Barney—all out here on the water. I didn't know if I was dreaming—but I ran all the way to 'Old Salty'—to find you. What has happened?"

He took a breath and looked bewildered and frightened.

"What has happened, Amy?" he said again. "Look at you. You are soaked and your face is bleeding. Is this Scarlet's doing as well? Where is she?"

Amy's dad turned his head towards the back of the boat. His face crumpled and his eyes filled with tears.

"Heavens, Helen," he said with a sob, "you're injured too."

Helen stood, reached forward and took David's hand as he stepped in next to her. He pulled another rope from 'Old Salty' and continued with his struggle to join the two boats together. His voice became desperate.

"You are all so wet and cold," he said. "Why are you

all out on the water in this terrible weather? I don't understand. My goodness," his voice broke. "Peter. He looks...he looks..."

Barney jumped up and barked. David slumped down next to Mum, put his head in his hands and stared forward. His eyes were wide with shock at the scene before him.

"It's all right," said Mum, gently. "We are all safe now. Scarlet has gone. Scarlet is dead."

The two boats bobbed quietly together on the water for many minutes. No-one spoke.

Amy could not believe how weak she felt. Peter lay quietly but peacefully, his hand still in hers.

Barney had bundled himself under one of the wooden seats and was quiet, although his eyes were still full of terror.

David had taken off his thick yellow boating jacket and wrapped it tightly around Helen. His arm was strong around her shoulders and he pulled her close to him.

A sense of quiet relief settled over them as they gradually tried to regain their strength.

At once, however, the sky darkened again, and thunder began to rumble in the distance. One strong zig-zag of lightning flew spectacularly across the horizon.

David stood up. "We need to get back to dry land," he said. "Otherwise the storm is going to be upon us."

Amy struggled to pull herself up onto one of the seats but wondered if she and Peter had the strength to stand.

"Come on," said Dad. "Let's all try to climb into the other boat. It will take us more quickly than trying to row."

But just as he finished speaking, he was thrown violently forward and fell to his knees. The water beneath the two boats had begun to shake. The light that had entered the water from the pulse in Amy's hand was now widening, and the sea was becoming increasingly turbulent and bright. With horror, Amy could now feel the unmistakeable presence of Scarlet.

Helen tightened her lips and pushed her hair back roughly with one hand, showing the injury to the side of her head and the wide streak of dried blood where it had run down her face.

"Something isn't right," she said. But her voice was strong. Her face was set in an expression of defiance and her eyes became wide as she leaned over the side of the boat and stared into the water, now rippling with dazzling and sparkling light.

The boats began to tilt and rock.

Amy held tightly onto Peter's hand and David pushed himself up from the bottom of the boat, his eyes looking wild with fear. He steadied himself and looked at Helen.

Her eyes locked onto his.

"The fight isn't over," she said, her voice strong with grim determination.

Near one end of the boat, a dark shape began to rise from the sea, and it kept rising. It was the shape of a slender woman. The hair was twisting and corkscrewing around the white face, the eyes wide but unafraid—the red mouth in a lopsided smirk and the arms flailing in a weird dance.

It was Scarlet. The beautiful, evil, terrible Scarlet. Alive.

Her body kept rising until she towered above them, higher than trees, higher than buildings, higher than mountains. The monstrous figure of Scarlet seemed to reach up and up—a terrifying version of herself—as far as the enormous dark clouds. She screeched and screamed with triumphant laughter.

CHAPTER 47

Angels

The sky was as dark as night. Thunder crashed overhead, and lightning zipped manically across the sky.

Helen stood up, David's jacket falling from her shoulders.

Amy cried out but her voice was lost in the confusion. Barney howled.

Amy's mother shouted defiantly. Then she reached forward and, seemingly without effort, picked up one of the huge heavy oars.

"Come on, David," she shouted. "Come on."

She swung powerfully with the oar towards the giant figure towering above them. Her face was red with the effort, but she swung and swung again.

"You evil hag," Helen screamed, her voice almost unrecognisable. "I know now. I know what you have done. You took my sister. You took my dearest Janice." Her voice was screeching. She lunged again with the oar. It struck the body of Scarlet and a fearful, terrible cry mixed with the thunder. She lunged again.

"And you took Amy." The oar swept again with unbelievable force against the legs of Scarlet. The giant body was too slow to react. She was struck and struck again.

The sky lightened briefly, and Amy could see clearly that the face of Scarlet had changed. The smirk had vanished, but an evil sneer had taken its place.

David grabbed the other oar and attacked Scarlet's body.

And then a huge, mighty plume of dark water began to rise from the surface of the boiling sea. Scarlet's outstretched arm was dragging it up. The strong slender fingers were forcing it to rise up and up to the same fearful height as herself. And then the water started pouring down onto the boat. It came in huge torrents, soaking them, taking their breath away and beginning to rapidly flood the boat at their feet and legs.

Helen and David stood and fought with Scarlet until the torrents of water pouring onto them forced them to surrender. The oars crashed down and they both fell, drenched and exhausted, into the bottom of the flooded boat.

Amy pushed herself up and away from the water and dragged Peter with her.

Peter started to whisper through the torrents of water that were almost smothering him.

"Clarke," he said very quietly and then his voice grew stronger until he was shouting.

"Clarke, CLARKE."

And then, a strong new sound was upon them in amongst all the terrifying confusion of the crushing hellish water. A sound like birds. The very loud sound of wings. The huge and beautiful white wings of the girls. And the powerful dark outstretched wings of Clarke.

Clarke's dear face rose gently as he soared upwards. The murky darkness in the column of water began to fade. Clarke and all the angelic forms of the lost girls flew up, their soft feathered wings beating in unison with a tremendous and wonderful sound.

They grasped Scarlet and dragged her, struggling and screaming into the raging plume of water. The enormous body began to shrink—smaller and smaller and the water fell relentlessly onto her terrified face with huge and terrible force. Her screams were swamped but still she struggled violently. They held her. They held her and held her until her strength faded and her body slumped forward. Still they held on. They held her lifeless body until they were sure. And then the column of water came roaring downwards and plunged into the sea.

Clarke and the girls flew on. Up and up and forever up until the beating wings were tiny specks. They dropped Scarlet's body from high in the sky. She fell and fell and then finally entered the dark sea with hardly a whisper and was lost forever.

The sound of the beating wings returned above them. Clarke and all the girls swooped across them in a beautiful and elegant circle. Clarke soared briefly amongst them and then, with the soft edge of one of his strong wings, he stroked Peter's pale head. They performed a beautiful and graceful dance in the air and then they swept away into the distance and were gone.

CHAPTER 48

Boats

The storm was over. The sky brightened and sun shone through the broken grey clouds in strong rays, lighting up the sea and making the crests of tiny waves sparkle and twinkle.

David and Helen reached forward and pulled Peter towards them. His clothes were soaked, and he shivered violently. David wrapped him in his jacket and they both hugged him until he was warm.

Barney jumped up, struggled and swam through the

deep water in the bottom of the boat to Amy and licked
her face.

Amy found the strength to sit up properly and to hug
his soft black neck.

"It's over," said David. "It seems like a terrible
nightmare but it's over."

Everything was still and quiet apart from the sound
of water as it sloshed inside the boat and the sea slapped
gently against the wooden hull.

"Mum, Dad," said Amy, her voice still weak. "You were
amazing. Amazing."

Mum nodded and closed her eyes. Dad pushed his
mouth into a strange smile. For a few minutes they were
all quiet again. And it felt good.

*

From stillness and quietness, they were now surrounded by
boats and people shouting.

Amy looked towards them with relief and
thankfulness. Many strong hands came quickly alongside.
They could see immediately that Amy and Peter were too
weak to stand. Buckets and scoops quickly baled the water
from the boat until it was almost gone.

One of the women untied the knots in the ropes
keeping the two small boats together. She invited Helen
and David to travel with her, but they said they would
rather stay with Peter and Amy. The woman understood.

She started the engine, took the wheel and circled around to collect the other boat, one oar dangling over the side and the other hidden at the bottom where it had been thrown down in such fury by Scarlet.

A rope was attached to the front of their boat by one of the rescuers. An engine roared in a more powerful boat, the water swirled and boiled and, before long, with several others alongside, they arrived at the steps of the quayside, 'Old Salty' bobbing along behind them on another rope.

Barney jumped into the arms of a young woman who had been driving the large boat with the engine. An ambulance appeared on the road at the top of the steps. A man and a woman jumped out and came forward with a stretcher.

"I can see definite casualties here," said the ambulance woman. "Who is in need of medical treatment?"

Amy sat up and her father lifted her gently into his arms. "We are cold and wet and shocked," he said. "But we will recover as soon as we are warm. Please take Peter to hospital. He has been…" and then he paused. "He has been very badly affected and will need time and care to recover."

Everyone was silent as a stretcher was taken into the boat, Peter was strapped in and gently carried up the steps.

CHAPTER 49

Sleep

B ack at the Craythorpes' house, Helen snuggled Amy into bed and very gently bathed her injured cheek. She drifted off to sleep almost immediately and slept for more than twenty hours.

When she finally woke, her mother and father were sitting by her bedside. Her first words were concern for Peter.

Amy's father reassured her that he was already out of hospital, in no danger and in a deep sleep in his bed down the corridor.

Amy sat up and reached to touch the injury on the side of Mum's head. David had tended to it and the cuts looked better—much better than she had expected. Then, she felt the jagged gashes on her own cheek. She carefully inspected her hand. The blue line to the tip of her finger was no longer there.

There were no surges of power pulsing through her body. She felt calm and peaceful. She almost felt like the Amy Harrington she had been before Scarlet had arrived, before the terrible events of the past days. Before Scarlet had tried to murder her. Before Scarlet had almost succeeded.

She looked into the worried eyes of her parents.

"I think I am myself again," she said quietly.

There was a tiny scratch at the door. It slowly opened and the black furry bundle of Barney came bounding in.

Amy, David and Helen were laughing and crying and hugging—with Barney jumping amongst them and joining in by rolling around on the bed.

And then Amy talked quietly to them about what had happened after she and Scarlet had left Boswell in the taxi, when her parents, still under Scarlet's spell, had so confidently waved them off. David and Helen sat open-mouthed and horrified as the story unfolded but they didn't once question it. They knew for certain that the terrible power of Scarlet had almost robbed them of Amy. And they also knew for certain that Scarlet was now destroyed. Destroyed by those she had so horribly wronged.

They hugged again.

Amy was exhausted by the telling of the terrible events that she had endured. Helen and David brought her food and left her alone for a long time to rest.

*

Amy knew that the powers, so briefly bestowed upon her, were now entirely gone. Every ounce of their strength had saved Peter's life. A few brief moments of confusion clouded her mind, but this was followed by a feeling of overwhelming relief. As the minutes ticked by, safe in her bed, she felt that, right now, she must be the happiest person in the whole world.

CHAPTER 50

Ordinary

After her very long rest, Amy was soon dressed and ready to go outside. The previous weakness she had felt had finally left her and she felt better. Barney jumped up and down at the promise of a walk.

They slowly crossed the temporary bridge over the river and then on towards Amy's house. She glanced across to the place where the grotesque figure of Scarlet had, only yesterday, been screaming. She shivered at the thought of it.

The powers she had generated to repair the house now felt unreal to her. She stretched out her arm, closed her eyes and tried to summon any strength, but there was nothing but her own normal muscles clenching and unclenching.

She heard a quiet voice behind her and turned. It was Peter. He looked pale and his blue eyes had a distant look.

Amy quickly crossed to where he was standing next to the wall of a tall grey house.

"Peter," she said. "Look at you. You are well. You are alive."

And then she laughed as Barney jumped up and down between them, barking excitedly.

"We are free, Peter. We are free. You saved my life, you saved Mum, you saved Barney. You saved us, Peter."

She looked into his eyes. "My powers are gone," she said. "I am glad. I am so glad to be ordinary again."

Peter turned from her and then leaned back against the grey wall. Amy hugged him, and he quietly sobbed into her shoulder. Amy let him cry until he finally breathed deeply.

"You saved my life, Amy. But all your powers have gone," he said. "That's the price you have paid for bringing me back from being…" but he couldn't say the word. "You could have done so much good in the world. I'm sorry."

"Don't be sorry," she said. "The powers were never what I wanted, Peter, but they have changed me for good, I am no longer the frightened little girl I once was. To have been so special would have been a terrible burden."

Peter grinned. "Amy, you are perfect. You don't need

powers. You are wonderful just as you are." But then his face clouded over. "What is to become of me?"

"Peter," she said. "My parents and I have discussed it. If you agree, you will be welcome to join our family and live with us and be like a brother to me. I can't believe it. I am so lucky to have found you."

Peter took a deep breath, his eyes widened, and he smiled broadly. He took Amy's hand and together, with Barney, they walked across to the house and peered in through the windows.

"There's still a lot to be done," said Peter. "But if we all work hard together, we should be soon be able to move in."

A gruff voice shouted from across the river. They turned and a man in a cap was waving at them. Amy recognised him as a friend of her father.

"Hey," he shouted. "Workmen have done a good job fixing up your house, young Amy. A brilliant job. I wonder if they will come over and have a look at mine?"

Peter and Amy stared at him for a moment and then at each other before bursting into laughter. And they laughed all the way back to the Craythorpes'.

CHAPTER 51

Recovery and Repair

The next few weeks went past quickly with everyone in the village working hard to repair all the damage of the flood. Peter's strength was fully restored, and he put all his energies into helping Amy, Helen and David to sort out the house. He was excellent at everything he turned his hand to. Clarke had taught him well.

Amy spent a lot of time describing much more about what had happened. It all began to feel like a bad dream. She was also eager to hear her mum talking about Janice, even though it made them both feel sad.

"She was a wonderful sister," Helen remembered, her eyes moist with tears.

"I know, Mum," said Amy. "I'm so sorry that Scarlet's cruelty and greed took her away from you. But, in a way, the beauty and strength of Janice and all the lost girls are within us now and we will take them forward into our own lives."

Helen smiled at this thought. She knew it would help her to heal, knowing that all the lost girls were with them in spirit.

CHAPTER 52

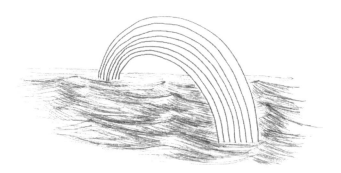

Yellow Petals

The house was finally ready and just in time for a visit from Angel, Delia and Madge. They arrived unexpectedly with a wish to do something special in memory of their dear friend, Clarke.

Peter and Amy invited them to walk down to the harbour where they told them about Clarke and the lost girls appearing in the water.

"Are you sure?" asked Delia. "You are saying that ghosts came to help you?"

But Madge and Angel nodded.

"Clarke was an amazing man," said Angel. "I'm not surprised at all that he brought the young girls to help save you, Amy."

It was only then that Amy realised that Angel was right. Clarke had been the one to awaken the souls of the girls and they had come together to take Scarlet into the deathly struggle with the water. To end her terrible curse.

"I've collected yellow rose petals," Madge was saying with a soft smile. "Yellow roses were always Clarke's favourite. Did you see how many there were in the garden, Amy?"

The five of them stepped into 'Old Salty'. Peter sat next to the small engine, his hand on the tiller.

He steered out to the scene where the beautiful ghosts had appeared.

"I believe Clarke and the girls gave us the very last of their strength to help save us," said Amy.

They each scattered the delicate, sweet smelling petals onto the gentle waves, closed their eyes and thought of all the goodness that was Clarke and they remembered all the innocent girls whose lives Scarlet had cut short with such selfish and terrible cruelty.

At that moment the sun shone brightly and then, in the distance, the sky darkened. A few soft drops of rain fell gently onto the sad upturned faces, but they all smiled together in wonderment as a huge, amazing double rainbow arched across the sky.

Delia took the engine tiller from Peter and skilfully brought the boat back to the harbour wall.

Two people were approaching in the distance. As they got closer, Amy recognised the familiar figures of Charlotte and Simran.

Angel helped Peter to tie the boat up to a rusty metal ring on the harbour wall and they all began to make their way up the slimy steps to where Simran and Charlotte were waiting.

They politely introduced themselves to Madge and the girls and then, with their eyes shining and clapping their hands, they announced that Rushworth was quickly being repaired, and the school would be opening again in ten weeks or maybe even sooner.

"You will love Rushworth, Peter," said Simran. "We can't wait for you to start. What is your favourite subject?"

Peter thought for a moment. "Science," he said.

Amy laughed. "We've got a brilliant science teacher," she said. "Mr Carr is wonderful." And then she smiled, remembering. "When he's himself," she added.

"Our school will also soon be ready," Delia said. "The parts that were on fire have been knocked down and they are rebuilding. It will be even better than it was before."

Peter and Amy travelled to the station with Delia, Angel and Madge.

"Will we be good friends?" Delia said.

Peter grinned. "Of course," he said. "You must visit us whenever you want, and we can visit you."

262 AMY HARRINGTON & THE CURSE OF SCARLET

Madge took a deep breath.

"All that we were was Scarlet's doing," she said. "Her death is a relief to us. Thank you, Amy, for your courage and strength. For setting us free."

They waved out of the window until the train disappeared around the bend in the tracks.

"They are right," said Peter. "You have saved us all from the curse of Scarlet."

"I couldn't have done it without you," said Amy. "And Clarke and the lost girls."

Then she turned to look at him full in the face.

"Peter," she said, her eyes sparkling. "I am so very proud to think of you as my brother."

Peter's eyes shone. Then his face looked thoughtful.

"I wonder what Scarlet's aunt was like," he said. "I wonder if she was a good woman. Maybe a healer? In those days, I suppose special powers were thought of as witchcraft."

Amy nodded. "And Scarlet used her powers for evil in the belief that she was somehow getting revenge for the death of her aunt. But the world is such a beautiful place, isn't it, Peter? Our special powers really don't need to come from magic at all. We don't need to live forever. No-one is perfect, but as long as we try to be kind and brave and generous, they are powers enough and they will always shine through brightly. It's so wonderful to be ordinary and special at the same time."

CHAPTER 53

Home

B ack in her own repaired room, Amy lay happily on her bed. She could hear Peter humming quietly to himself in the next bedroom and her mum and dad laughing downstairs.

The curtains were open, and the sky was dark—with just the faint twinkle of a few stars. She stretched out her hand to feel the soft fringe of her bedside lampshade. It was comforting and soft.

The door crashed open and Barney came bounding in

with his funny grinning mouth, his ears flopping and his tongue lolling out. He jumped up onto the bed and into Amy's arms.

Everything felt the same but equally, everything felt different. She snuggled up to Barney for a long time and then stood up to close the curtains, looking again into the dark sky without a trace of fear. The landing clock chimed quietly.

Amy walked across to her little wardrobe and traced her finger slowly around the soft nose of Neddy-Knock-Knees.

"Hello, dearest Neddy," she said with a wide smile. "I'm back."

THE END